Also by Sheila Kohler

THE PERFECT PLACE

MIRACLES
IN AMERICA

MIRACLES
IN AMERICA

STORIES BY

SHEILA
KOHLER

Alfred A. Knopf · New York · 1990

THIS IS A BORZOI BOOK
PUBLISHED BY ALFRED A. KNOPF, INC.

Copyright © 1987, 1988, 1989, 1990 by Sheila Kohler

"In Amber," "Miracles in America," and "Via delle Rose" were originally published
in The Quarterly.

Library of Congress Cataloging in Publication Data
Kohler, Sheila.
Miracles in America : stories / by Sheila Kohler. — 1st ed.
p. cm.
ISBN 0-394-57374-9
I. Title.
PR9369.3.K64M5   1990
823—dc20   89-11222   CIP

Manufactured in the United States of America
First Edition

For Sasha,
Cybèle and Brett,
and for Bill

O Rose, thou art sick!
The invisible worm
That flies in the night,
In the howling storm,

Has found out thy bed
Of crimson joy,
And his dark secret love
Does thy life destroy.

WILLIAM BLAKE

CONTENTS

VIA DELLE ROSE

When Rachel left her husband of many years, she would hardly have said her life was beginning. She had no family, few friends; she was drinking too much; she was falling apart.

Sometimes, unable to read, she would sit immobile at the window, listening to the sound of the bells tolling the hour and watching the swallows circle above her like dark specks of dust stirred up in the white sky. She would imagine the faces of people she had once known and, sometimes, even that of some mysterious stranger, in the shapes of the passing clouds. Finally she would move, only to fill her glass and sink down on the bed, lying there heavily, restless, unable to sleep.

When the maid came in the morning she would find the bedroom door still closed. She moved quietly around the apartment, pushing a soft damp cloth on the end of a brush across the cold tiled floor.

The maid, who was one of six children, probably liked the thick walls of the villa where Rachel had rented a floor, on Via delle Rose, though there were no roses on that street. Perhaps what the maid liked was the shuttered quiet of the first floor—what was known as the *piano nobile*—and the sheltered, sunny veranda with its creepers and potted plants, which she watered diligently all through the Roman winter, humming love songs softly to herself as she worked, so as not to disturb Rachel.

Eventually, sometime before noon, Rachel would call out, "I'm awake, you can bring in breakfast," or she would say, "Gray day, isn't it, Rosetta?" her pale face glimmering for a moment at the door.

Rosetta, who was a slight girl with knock-knees and a fresh, country face, would walk quickly into the kitchen and tie her apron strings twice around her small waist.

The maid served Rachel her breakfast of bread and coffee, and fresh strawberries when she could find them, on a tray in her bed. Rosetta would fold back the shutters, letting the sunlight into the room, and stand by the bed, while inquiring with apparent interest after Rachel's health. There was something about Rachel's daily description of her constitution, of her sleepless nights, a certain exotic quality, reinforced by the accented Italian, that probably fascinated Rosetta.

"I couldn't sleep for hours," Rachel might say, and wave a ringed hand, impatiently, in the air.

Rosetta would turn to Rachel and cluck her tongue with sympathy, though she could, no doubt, hardly imagine lying awake in a bed; when, her endless chores accomplished, she managed to get into hers, she always fell asleep immediately.

"My head aches terribly. My liver is shot already, and the doctors tell me it'll be the end of me if I go on drinking. But sometimes, when I wake in the morning and find all of myself still there—the arms, the legs, the head—you know, Rosetta, I have the feeling I'd really rather never wake again," Rachel would say, and laugh in her brittle way, and bring the conversation to an end, delicately wiping the froth of the whipped milk from the fine, dark hair of her upper lip with her lace handkerchief.

Occasionally, she would continue.

"*Tout casse, tout lasse, tout passe*," she might say, or something of the sort, and vague images of her past would come to her: the sun on a stone wall, a white azalea on a mantelpiece, a blue silk dressing gown hanging behind the bathroom door.

But she felt little, only the headache and the fear of not being able to sleep.

"My father almost died of a heart attack last winter," Rosetta might say, and shake all her thin fingers from her narrow wrist like leaves on a branch in the wind.

Rachel would chew on a piece of toast in the side of her mouth, as though the business of eating were distasteful to her. Or she picked at the luscious strawberries with her small, plump fingers, holding up the dead-ripe fruit to the light. Sometimes Rachel spoke with increasing bitterness, her voice rising. She spoke of her husband—his continuous infidelity; of men in general—their conceit, their cowardice; of the human race—its abuse of any position of power. Occasionally she ended by upbraiding Rosetta herself for some minor misdemeanor, shouting at her. She even accused the maid of stealing a silk blouse, which Rachel had probably forgotten she had given her. Once, at the height of her helpless furor, Rachel brought her fist down on the rose pattern of the plate, shattering the pottery, which flew across the floor in small pieces.

During all of this, Rachel was aware of the hopelessness of trying to explain to Rosetta whatever it was she was actually trying to explain. Often, with tears in her eyes, she concluded by simply grasping the maid's hand and squeezing her fingers and then sending the maid from the room precipitately. Afterward, Rachel would apologize for her outburst and ask Rosetta not to mention it to anyone.

"*A nessuno, non lo dirò a nessuno,*" Rosetta would say. Naturally the maid told all the people in the palazzo that the American signora was mad, really quite out of her mind. The people in the palazzo began to treat Rachel with studied politeness when they met her on the steps. As for Rachel herself, she continued to sit at the window and watch the winter sky, waiting for spring.

The boy appeared as if by magic, like a frangipani bloom on a gray, leafless branch. Rachel had known his mother at school, a long time before. When the mother telephoned to say the boy was looking for a place to stay, Rachel imagined a small boy in short velvet pants—a red-cheeked, curly-headed child with a wide mouth and wide-spaced blue eyes.

But he was not a child at all, though he was not yet full grown. He stood with one foot behind the other, angular, almost bony, his chin lifted. He wore a gold earring dangling rakishly from one ear and his fair hair was cropped close to his head, so that the bones of his face seemed almost angry, and his hair stood up, bristling about him.

He had, Rachel thought, the fresh, flushed cheeks of a young girl.

Perhaps it was because of the pale spring light on the veranda, or the odor of damp earth that rose from the dripping, tangled back gardens below, but the boy seemed quite beautiful to Rachel, particularly his eyes, which were large, dark blue, acquisitive, but at the same time sad.

"Why did you come to Rome?" Rachel asked.

"For the experience," the boy said almost challengingly.

She ought to have changed out of her white shirt, Rachel thought, rubbing at a spot on the cuff.

"Friend of mine came here last summer. I won't tell you what happened to him," the boy added.

"What did happen to him?" Rachel asked.

"Actually, I only know what they say happened," the boy said. He lowered his gaze, gave Rachel a quick glance, and then lowered his eyes again. He was not as beautiful as his mother had been, but something incongruously girlish about the boy's face made Rachel smile.

As Rachel turned to show the boy the way down the steps and into the passageway, his arm brushed accidentally against hers, and she drew back abruptly.

Rachel asked the boy how his mother was.

"Actually, she was against Rome. She wanted me to go to the beach," he said.

Rachel felt the tears come into her eyes. "I'll show you the room," she said, and opened the door.

The room had no view, but looked over the quiet dark well of a courtyard. It was small but comfortably furnished—though, just then, somewhat in disorder.

The boy hesitated, standing on the threshold, checked, perhaps, by the fact that the bedcovers had been thrown back, exposing piles of freshly laundered intimate apparel. It was a room that Rosetta sometimes used in the afternoons for the ironing.

"I told the maid to tidy this room," Rachel said, and swept up a pile of laundry with an angry gesture. I'll have to do something about Rosetta, Rachel thought. The maid seemed to feel it was sufficient to push the duster across the floor and make the breakfast.

The boy stepped into the room and sat down on the bed, looking around. "I like it as it is," he said, bouncing up and down on the mattress.

Rachel glanced at him uneasily.

When the boy had left to fetch his things, Rachel tied a scarf around her head and dusted the room thoroughly. She smoothed the sheets across the bed, letting her hand linger a moment on the pillow slip.

"He's seventeen," Rachel said the next morning.

"Big," Rosetta said. She made a fist and shook it in the air as she added, "Well developed for his age, is it not true?"

Rachel was thinking of his mother's smooth brown legs.

Rosetta shifted from one small foot to the other and sighed. She asked Rachel if she would be responsible for the boy's laundry, his room. Would she have to make his bed? Would the boy eat in the house? "He's going to need some taking care of," Rosetta concluded glumly.

"That's true," Rachel replied slowly, as though the thought had just occurred to her, and finished her cup of coffee.

Rachel walked slowly across the sunlit room to the window.

The sky was a clear blue, the outline of the red roofs distinct. She filled her lungs with air easily and stood there, her hands on the windowsill, feeling almost dizzy, her dusky skin lit up.

Rachel had not been a beautiful adolescent. Her skin was too sallow, her cheeks too round—she couldn't resist sweet things— and her hands always slightly clammy. Her dark eyes seemed sullen, though they lit up from time to time unexpectedly. Her thick, wavy chestnut hair, which she caught back in a loose knot perched precariously at the nape of her neck, was her best feature. She wore clothes that were too tight for her, dressing untidily in shirts that had a way of riding up out of the waist of her clinging linen skirts.

She had wanted to be a journalist but was very soon impatient with the tedium of the profession. She married an Italian she met on an assignment instead, believing she had fallen passionately in love with him, losing ten pounds and abandoning her work.

The man, an impoverished aristocrat from Urbino, was probably fascinated by a certain sensuality in Rachel's movements, the smoldering quality of her gaze, the way she draped herself across a deck chair with heavy lassitude, and by her fortune, which was considerable, acquired by her father in the diamond business. Besides, she courted the count with insistence and married him despite—or, perhaps, partly because of—her family's strong disapproval.

This was how Rachel's father expressed his opinion of his new son-in-law: "Count No-account," he said, and gave his daughter a liberal allowance but told her he no longer wanted her in his house. When he died, he left Rachel his fortune and a spectacular collection of diamonds, some of which she kept in the top drawer of her dresser.

Rachel's mother said, "An Italian, a Catholic. He'll give all your money to the Pope; he'll make you bring your children up as Catholics," and muttered something darkly about nuns burying babies in the backs of convent gardens.

Anyway, Rachel remained childless, took good care of her fortune, and spent her time watching over her husband, jealously waiting for the first signs of infidelity.

Once, when her husband came back late at night, he found Rachel roaming the streets without a coat, looking for him. He caught sight of her and stood watching her for a moment in the shadows as she came toward him, hugging the walls, coming on with something wild and purposeful in her gait. It had begun to rain, a fine mist of rain, falling like dust under the lamplight. Rachel, when she saw the count, stopped still, with her thick hair falling loose around her face in restless curls, the rain on her face, her big, dark eyes lit up with anger, her shiny dress clinging to her heavy breasts.

"You know what you remind me of?" he said.

She raised her dark eyebrows in inquiry.

"Salome," he said and laughed.

The boy did not seem particularly shy. He came and went to his classes with his books under his arm, concentrating, apparently, on his studies.

Two nights after he had moved in, Rachel watched him in the hall preparing to go out. He stood before the mirror, brushed his cropped hair back with the tips of his fingers, and then swung his leather jacket over his shoulder.

Rachel asked him if he would like to eat with her. "It must be expensive eating out all the time," she said.

He turned his head sharply and replied, "No thanks," so firmly it startled her. "If I eat with you once, I'll end up doing it every night," he said.

Rachel and Rosetta walked down the stone steps of the palazzo together.

Before the maid turned down a side street, Rachel caught her looking up at the darkening sky and then casting a quick, furtive glance back at her mistress, who went on walking down Via delle Rose, the wind blowing her hair into her eyes.

The maid was really afraid of her, Rachel thought. Rosetta had probably told the whole palazzo her mistress was a drunk, although these days Rachel had been drinking less. Since the boy had been in the house, Rachel often left the apartment in the afternoons, walking slowly into the center of Rome, strolling through the sunlit streets, stopping to look up at the arch and curve of a baroque church or letting her hand run under the cool water of a fountain on the corner of a street. Sometimes she climbed up to the Campidoglio to watch the sun set over the city, or lingered for a moment on the Spanish Steps, gazing down at the boat-shaped fountain below. Occasionally she even went as far as St. Peter's. She wandered around the vast church, her eyes lifted, taking in the smell of incense, the color of the cardinal's robes, the way the light came slantingly through the alabaster window. Once, she found herself covering her hair and genuflecting before an altar, crossing herself as the other women did, and then kneeling down in the shadows in silence—not praying, her eyes on the sweep of the gold baldachin, a bowed dark head, the curve of a white marble bust.

Occasionally, on certain warm evenings, she did not go home for dinner but sat under the creeper of some outdoor trattoria, eating a plate of *spaghetti in bianco* and watching the swallows circle in the transparent blue sky.

She found herself avoiding the boy. She could hear him in the mornings banging away in the kitchen, getting his breakfast—probably spilling the milk, she thought—or coming in late at night well past midnight and playing his transistor radio loudly in his room.

He asked her questions too, rather rudely, she felt, questions like: "What do you *do* all day?" "Don't you ever get bored?" "Have you *never* worked?" "Do you drink *whiskey* every night?"

And she didn't drink whiskey every night, she thought now, as she felt the first heavy drops of rain on her face. She turned then and retraced her steps. She would get her umbrella, she decided, going back up the stone steps slowly. She would go for a long walk in the rain. She had never minded the rain; in fact, she rather liked the sudden summer storms, the excitement of it all.

The rain began to fall heavily as she opened the door to the apartment. She could hear the rain coming down hard while she stood looking around for her umbrella. She noticed that her bedroom door was ajar. She was certain she had closed the door. She was almost certain she had locked it.

She walked quietly across the tiled floor of the living room, breathing heavily. She felt hot, and she was perspiring, her hands damp, as she pushed open the door.

In the gray, flickering light of the storm, the boy stood before the open drawer of her dresser, bending over slightly, with his back to her. She could see the back of his round, cropped head, like a fist.

"*What* are you doing?" she said.

When the boy turned and saw Rachel's face, he took two steps back, ducking his head to one side, as if to avoid a blow.

"How dare you!" Rachel yelled, her rage coming to her slowly as if from afar. As Rachel advanced on the boy, one arm raised to strike him, she could feel her head throbbing like the rain pounding on the window. The light seemed ashen around the boy, his smile coming and going across his face, his blue eyes dark, a deep violet. Suddenly he turned and bolted, so quick on his feet he startled Rachel, and she drew back.

The two women sat in the kitchen under the glare of the yellow light, listening to the sound of the rain and the ticking of the kitchen clock, waiting for the boy.

It was late, and he had been gone a long time.

"Perhaps I should go down into the street to see if I can find him. Where do you suppose he goes at night? Do you imagine he has a girl, or do you think he goes with the prostitutes?" Rachel asked.

Rosetta went on cleaning the silver cup with her thin pink hands. She rubbed at the silver with slow, mechanical gestures, without looking up, shrugging her shoulders and pulling down the edges of her mouth and saying only *"Beh"* when Rachel looked at her inquiringly.

The maid was really no help, Rachel thought. She seemed to get slower and slower. From time to time, Rachel had found her just standing in the middle of a room, her wide mouth slightly open, a duster in her hand. Perhaps the maid was really a little touched in the head.

"Didn't you just clean that silver, Rosetta?" Rachel asked.

"It passes the time, signora," the maid said.

Rachel lifted her gaze to the ceiling.

There was a long pause.

Rachel said suddenly, pouring herself another drink, "Perhaps I should call his mother."

"What would you say to the signora?" Rosetta replied, looking up for a moment from the silver cup, blinking her clear gray eyes.

Rachel gave the maid a glance of surprise, because, after all, what on earth *would* she say to the mother? Even more to the point, she was afraid of what the mother might say to her, Rachel. The mother would be sure to ask what the boy was doing in the dresser drawer, and what *was* the boy doing in the dresser drawer? Perhaps he was simply looking for something—a pencil or a stamp. Or perhaps he simply wanted to see her things. Perhaps he was just curious.

"Would you like me to make some camomile tea?" Rosetta

asked, sniffed, and went on polishing. She was on the spoons now, taking each one and holding it up to the light to make sure it was thoroughly clean.

Rachel shook her head, poured another whiskey, and indicated the tissues on the shelf. The maid blew her nose loudly.

Rachel looked at her face and thought suddenly that her skin looked almost transparent, and that she was getting thinner. Her face was pinched. Her nose looked bony and a little red. Her big red mouth and her blank gray eyes seemed to take up all of her small face. Her striped uniform, though clean, hung on her shoulders. She was not an ugly girl, Rachel thought, but she'd probably never find a husband, poor thing. Rachel wasn't quite sure what it was the maid lacked, something like vitality. There was a vagueness about Rosetta, a certain passivity, a sort of resignation that irritated Rachel. When Rosetta had first come from the country to work for her, Rachel had found her fresh-looking and neat. She had grown quite fond of her. But the maid seemed to have lost her color in the town, to have grown absentminded in her work. Perhaps I have spoiled her, Rachel thought.

Rachel had a sudden desire to get up and take the maid by her shoulders and give her a good shake. Instead, she sighed and said, "Not that I really know very much about the boy. He's been in this house for over a month, and I know next to nothing about him. He doesn't say much. Keeps to himself most of the time, doesn't he? Who knows, perhaps he takes something, or he's got mixed up with some gang of thugs. Perhaps he's got some girl into trouble."

Rosetta put the spoon down and said in a voice as monotonous as the sound of the rain, "A cousin of mine fell into the hands of the Mafia. Never heard from him again."

"Good heavens," Rachel said and shuddered. She added, "Of course anything's possible these days. But he always looks so innocent to me, isn't it true? It's those blue eyes. He has beautiful eyes, don't you think? He looks, not naïve, but innocent. And he has the soft skin of a girl. Have you ever noticed his skin?"

The maid shrugged her shoulders and pulled her mouth down at the corners and said, *"Beh?"* lifting her hands, palms up, to the ceiling.

Rachel said, "If you say '*beh*' once more, I'll scream."

Rosetta didn't say anything but kept on polishing, her eyes lowered.

There was a long silence. Then Rachel said, "How could I have known?" letting her head sink down into her arms.

She felt ill. Her head ached terribly. She had a pain down her side which might be the liver, she thought. She shouldn't have drunk so much whiskey. She thought of the Italian doctor, an elderly man with silver hair, saying to her, "You cut out alcohol absolutely or . . ." snapping his long white fingers with an eloquent gesture in the air, looking grave. She had known exactly what he meant. She could even imagine it: her life going from her as easily as the snap of the doctor's white fingers.

Rachel lifted her head slightly and propped it on one hand and whispered, "Perhaps something terrible has happened to the boy, perhaps he's been hurt, perhaps he's lying somewhere, wounded, dead." She sat up completely and said dramatically, looking at Rosetta directly, clenching both fists, "Do you know, Rosetta, if I could have, I think I might almost have killed him at that moment."

"My father once almost killed one of my brothers, beat him to within an inch of his life," Rosetta said in her deadpan voice, as though killing people were the most ordinary thing in the world, and went on polishing the knives.

"Oh, for God's sake, Rosetta, stop polishing that silver, will you. I can't stand it any longer," Rachel said, and stood up and began pacing around the kitchen. She realized she was shouting. "Why don't you just go on home. Go on. Go home. There's really no point in your sitting there like a . . ." She tried to think of how to say "sack of potatoes" in Italian idiom and gave up. The worst was not being able to swear at the girl in English, she thought.

When the maid had gone, Rachel sat at the kitchen table and poured herself another drink.

A cat was crying on the landing, the howl rising and falling in the night. Rachel laid her head down on the table again. Useless, she thought. She would never sleep until she knew what had happened to the boy, not even if she drank an entire bottle of whiskey. There was a noise then, the rattle of a sudden gust of wind on the windowpane, or perhaps the action of a key in the lock. The rain had stopped. She turned toward the door.

The boy walked into the room. He was wet and breathing hard; he had probably been running; his eyes looked bloodshot. He stood at the other end of the kitchen table with his head hanging, his thin shoulders stooped, not looking at her but rubbing the tip of his finger on the table, catching his breath.

Rachel pushed back her loose hair from her face, adjusting her white gown over her breasts.

"I saw the light on in the kitchen, and I thought—" the boy said.

Rachel pulled the belt of her gown tighter around her waist and wet her lips.

The boy rubbed the oilcloth on the table, making it shine, but he wasn't looking at the table. Rachel watched his self-conscious movements.

"Do you want to sit down?" she asked.

The boy went on rubbing at a spot on the oilcloth. Then he crossed his arms across his chest, hugging himself, his head bowed. He'd got skinny in her house, Rachel thought.

"I suppose you're going to explain to me what you were doing?" Rachel said.

The silence between them was almost tangible. Rachel realized all her anger had gone now. She hunted for it, but she couldn't find it. Then, suddenly, she went to him and pressed his wet head to her shoulder. She stroked his head, feeling the stubby hair, the bones.

"It's all right," she whispered, hurriedly, senselessly.

He pulled away, looking down at her. "You don't understand. Please, don't talk," he hissed, his face close, his lips swollen, trembling. "When I saw the light on, I thought you might be worried. I didn't want to . . ." He drew back from her.

She remembered she had not brushed her hair or put any makeup on her face. He must smell the whiskey on her breath. All her wrinkles must be visible under the harsh kitchen light. She turned away and smoothed back her hair. She reached out to him again and pressed him close to her, pushing his head against her shoulder, feeling his warmth begin to spread through her body.

He hung there limply, his eyes shut, apparently exhausted.

"I love you," she said to the boy, with tears in her eyes, her hot whiskey breath on his neck.

"I shouldn't have come back. I was crazy," the boy said, but without moving, his body still resting against hers.

"I know how you must feel. I just wanted you to know."

"You don't know anything," the boy said and pulled away from her.

She had a pain down her side. She looked at the boy, who slumped now into the kitchen chair where Rosetta had sat, his head in his hands, the water dripping from the end of his nose.

She told him to go and take off his wet things. She asked him if he was hungry, if she could make him some food. She felt suddenly ravenous. She had eaten nothing since the day before at lunch, she realized. The boy shrugged his shoulders, but rose and went to his room. She could hear the sound of the shower as she began to cook: eggs, bacon, a huge pile of toast. She squeezed oranges and grapefruits. She brewed coffee and heated the milk. When she called the boy for breakfast, he was in his blue pajamas, his cheeks red, his hair sticking up around his head like a blond halo, Rachel thought.

She had laid the kitchen table with a clean white cloth and spread the breakfast out. The boy sat down and began to eat. He ate slowly at first, and then with increasing speed, one slice of toast after the other, three fried eggs—dipping the bread into the eggs, slices and slices of bacon with his fingers. Rachel sat and ate beside the boy, buttering the slices of toast in silence.

Through the kitchen window the sky grew light over the ancient city. The terra-cotta facades, the pink-and-white azaleas, the stray cats, the fountains, the stones of the churches emerged once again out of the night.

.   .   .

After that the summer months slipped by easily like smooth beads through the fingers of her hand, despite the heat, which gradually increased as they approached August. Afterward, Rachel thought that she could probably have gone on like that forever, almost happy.

She rose early, bathed, and dressed carefully in fresh cotton dresses with gaily colored high-heeled sandals and handbags to match. She went to market before the heat of the day. She bought bright fruits: strawberries, peaches, plums; vegetables and flowers; fish and meat. She touched the fruit and vegetables carefully, as she had seen the neighborhood Italian women do. She observed the eye of the fish to be certain of its freshness. She had the vendor cut into the watermelon and tasted a slice on the street, bending over so as not to spill the juice down the front of her dress. She came home laden down, her straw baskets filled. She cooked breakfast for the boy, even bringing him his eggs and bacon in bed on the weekends, with freshly squeezed juice and a flower on the tray.

The boy ate all his meals at home, eating copiously. He had an appetite that made Rachel laugh. She wondered how he had managed to feed himself all through the first month he had spent in her place.

In the long, hot afternoons they sat together on the veranda with the orange awning drawn down, casting a pinkish shade. The boy sat with his feet crossed on the railing of the veranda, his hands behind his head. Rachel helped him with his Italian. He left the book unopened on his knees and asked her for certain useful phrases.

At first he asked her for the exact names of the parts of the body, how to order a dinner, how to buy things in a shop. Eventually he asked her directly for words of love. Laugh-

ingly, she taught him what she had learned from the count.
Gradually they began to talk in Italian, the boy haltingly and
Rachel increasingly spontaneously. She told him about her
childhood, her friendship with his mother, her life with the
count.

"Now he was a good lover. Anything went," she said, and
opened up her arms in a gesture of acceptance.

The boy lifted his eyebrows appreciatively and smiled with
complicity.

Rachel wondered what he knew about the art of love.

In the autumn, when the boy had gone, Rachel took to walking
the streets alone, unable to sleep in the early mornings, amazed
at the industry at that early hour. In the shadows of the dawn,
the streets wet and glistening, bakers baked bread and butchers
cut up meat. She stopped once and watched, fascinated, while
a butcher with a bloodstained apron carried an entire carcass of
some animal over his shoulder. At times she realized she was
talking to herself, her lips moving silently.

One morning, when she came back from market to Via delle
Rose early, she went into the kitchen and found Rosetta already
there. The maid was sitting by the window in the sun, gazing
out at the bright sky, her dark hair tied back from her face,
her big mouth slightly open. She had thrown her head back
with her chin lifted, and the clear sunlight was on her face
and her chest. Her skin looked transparent. Rachel followed the
line of her neck to her full breasts and down to her thickened
waist.

The maid, seeing Rachel staring, started and got up. She
walked across the kitchen to Rachel slowly, awkwardly.

Rachel went on staring, her eyes on what she must have seen but not recognized before.

For a moment the two women stood in silence, facing one another, the maid looking down at the pool of sunlight on the tiled floor and Rachel looking down at her.

"Poor girl, poor dreamer," Rachel said, for the maid and for herself, and patted the maid on the shoulder.

THE FACTS

No, he would not tell her about it. It would only make her angry, and really, when she was angry, she quite frightened him. There was no other word for it. Her eyes flashed, and her hair—those lustrous curls—seemed quite wild, almost frizzy. She was not beautiful even then, but she was more beautiful than she usually was, lit up with anger, incandescent, *light in her hair and resentment in her heart*, and still frightening to him, quite awful in her wrath.

No, he would have to make something up to explain the lateness of the hour, he thought. He felt something wet and soft on his cheek and looked up at the familiar buildings, muffled now and made strange by the snow, it seemed to him, or perhaps by that indeterminate light between day and night. *Miles to go before I sleep*, he thought and lowered his head, sniffed the evening air, and hoped he had not caught cold. He tightened the belt to his raincoat with a careful hand and was glad he had remembered his galoshes.

The problem was that he was no good, had never been any good, at making things up, had always preferred, whenever it was possible, to stick to the facts. He had no trouble with facts. He was, he knew, awfully good with facts. He might even go as far as saying, he believed, and without boasting, that he was quite brilliant with facts. After all, there had been his scores on the entrance examinations for the universities; there had been his record at school; there had been the scholarships, the honors. All of that was due in part, he was sure, to his unusual ability to concentrate on the matter at hand, and all of that had taken place, he had to admit, some time ago. His excellent education—he was, after all, one of the few people he knew who could speak, let alone write, a grammatical sentence—had actually turned out to be a great burden to him. This knowledge of the language, of words, of the precise meaning of words, this almost total recall—pages of poetry coming to him at odd moments, obscure quotations, never anything anyone else could share, what he thought of as his mumbled poetical obscurities— had been nothing but a burden to him and certainly no help with his career, for who, these days, needed Chaucer or even Wordsworth, for that matter?

Still, he thought, and lifted his chin and straightened his back and even rose a little on the balls of his feet, that woman this evening had seemed very interested by the particular set of facts he had presented to her, and he smiled a little and almost laughed aloud. But then, he whispered to the evening air, *Athena and Aphrodite have always been intimately linked.*

As for her, as for his wife, he knew she was thoroughly disappointed with his performance. She told him often enough that he had not risen to the heights she had expected of him. She said she had expected him to be not only rich but also famous, and he was neither. Oh, they were well off, she had her fur coat and more clothes than she could wear, but he could not honestly call himself rich, and he was certainly not famous, and there was little chance of his becoming so at his age, he supposed, and then remembered, suddenly, the woman's gaze that evening as she leaned toward him, admiration in her eyes. What was it she had said? Was it, "Quite remarkable!" Or was it, rather, "Extraordinary, quite extraordinary!" For some reason he could not remember the woman's exact words, but he did remember what he had felt. For a moment he had felt like a Colossus—that was it. He had felt like a Colossus, and all the rest but petty men, walking beneath his feet. *The fault, dear Brutus, is not in our stars,* he thought, opening the door to the building and beginning the ascent of the stairs with sprightly step.

His wife, unfortunately, saw nothing remotely resembling a Colossus about him. She said, *the most unkindest cut of all,* that his little life limped sadly. She said he was dull, that he was interested only in facts. She said he knew nothing of feelings, or, at any rate, that he knew nothing of *her* feelings, that he never questioned her about her feelings, her conflicting, her fluctuating, her deepening feelings. She said he never asked her what she *felt.* And it was true. It was absolutely true. He never did ask her what she felt, because, quite honestly, he was afraid of what she might come up with, he was afraid of what she might say. She was quite capable of coming up with something that would make him grind his teeth and pluck at his cheek. She was quite capable of making him tremble all over his slight body. Did she not realize that he much preferred to remain in ignorance, that he much preferred not to know about her precious feelings?

Good heavens, half the time he preferred not to know what she told him, what she insisted on telling him without any sort of encouragement at all. My God, she was capable of telling him, and this in the middle of dinner, this in the middle of his savoring a particularly delicious meal at an expensive eating place, and on his birthday, that she would have liked to do it with that strapping, dark-haired man at the next table, with that man who laughed loudly and sat with his legs spread apart. She had told him, nudging him in the ribs and cocking her head to one side archly, in that way she had, and on these very stairs, told him that she would have liked to do it with that workman in his dirty, tight jeans. Well, he would rather not think about the tightness of those jeans.

No, as for him, he preferred to stick to plain facts. But he could hardly tell his wife that he was late because that woman had lingered, had taken such a long time about her business, and he, under the circumstances, had not considered it was in his interest to be rude, had not considered it was in his interest to rush her at such an important moment, at what he might, after all, even call a crucial moment. He could hardly tell his wife that not only had he not wanted to rush the woman but that he had wanted to hold onto the moment, that the whole experience—he must have been with the woman in that small room for over half an hour—had given him that sudden sense of becoming, well yes, what came to mind was still the Colossus.

His wife would not understand. She would be put off, or, and the thought made him shudder, worse still, she might even sneer, she might simply sit there and tilt her lovely head back and laugh at him, laugh that deep-throated laugh of hers. She might say, he imagined, "You, of all people! You with that holier-than-thou look on your face!" She might say, "Good God, of all the men in the world. Not you!" He did not think he would be able to bear that. No, he could hardly go and tell his wife something of that sort, knowing it was exactly the sort of thing that would be likely to infuriate her or even to fill her with contempt.

Well, at least he had the food, he thought, climbing the stairs slowly now, clutching the heavy brown paper bag to his chest with both his hands and smelling the innumerable dinners cooking or long since cooked and sitting congealing on the backs of greasy stoves. At least he had that nice piece of fish and the onions he could fry up with some potatoes, perhaps. He was, he considered, particularly good with fried potatoes. Even his wife said that he was very good with fried potatoes. She might like his fried potatoes tonight, he thought, that is, if she had not gone off already, if she had not flounced out of the door in that flashy green dress—oh my God!—the one with the buttons down the front, the one that had cost him a week's pay, going off to some expensive place and eating and drinking just enough, considering that each item cost what those items do, to let him know how she felt, charging it all on the credit card, so that he would have to pay with his hard-earned cash.

Even if she had gone off to some restaurant, she would be back, eventually. She always came back, eventually, not having at her disposal, he supposed, anywhere better to go, not having found an apartment with more space or a better view or more light than their reasonable, sunny, and spacious apartment in a very good part of town, not having found anywhere better to stay or anyone else who would pay as constantly and as consistently as he did for her various undertakings: the history degree, followed by the pottery classes, which then became the sudden interest in art, the night classes at art school, the artists with whom she considered it would be necessary for her to sleep if she was to advance her career, and which he should not object to if he really loved her and wanted her to be happy, after all.

Whatever the reason was, he knew, she would come back, and she would want, would insist upon, some sort of explanation, an explanation that, he realized, he had better prepare ahead of time and not leave to chance or to some sort of last-minute inspiration, knowing full well that he was not very good at having last-minute inspirations and that, even when he did have them, she was sure to see through them.

No, he could definitely not leave it up to last-minute inspiration, because heaven knew what might come to him in the way
of inspiration. He was afraid of that, too. He was afraid of what
he might say, had always been afraid that he might say something inappropriate, might come up with something all too re-
vealing, might stand up in a house of worship and shout out
something obscene, he thought, and propped the heavy bag on
his knee while he hunted for his latchkey, almost dropping the
fish and listening for sounds from within, deciding at the same
time as he found his key that there was no solution to the
problem, that he would just have to tell her, that he would just
have to go ahead and tell her about the woman's enthusiasm,
that he would just have to tell her that because of the woman's
enthusiasm, the woman's interest in the matter at hand, the
woman's interest in those facts he had presented to her, the sort
of facts that had always seemed to him, though never to his wife,
highly stimulating, the business had taken much longer than he
would have thought.

He stepped into the room. He stood silent and pale before his
wife, who was reading on the sofa, her legs crossed. She lifted
her head. She dropped her book, stood up, and walked toward
him slowly in the flashy green dress and the high heels. Her hair
glowed. She stood beside him and stared him in the eyes. For a
moment he thought she was going to strike him. Then she said,
"I think you had better sit down. There is something I have to
tell you."

MIRACLES IN AMERICA

It was not something you could actually see, not something you would ever want to see, so they didn't notice it for the longest time. They were very young, too—neither the boy nor the girl had turned twenty-one—and probably they were not used to noticing much.

As a matter of fact, they were not the ones who finally noticed it, when it was finally noticed. It was the grandmother who noticed first, and not only noticed but told everyone about it; it was the grandmother who, you might say, opened up the box and let the devils loose. Not that, even then, they recognized the devils as such that summer in Italy down by the sea.

It took the years to do that.

It was a hot, breathless summer on the Italian Riviera. The wind was dead calm, the Mediterranean like a lifeless lake. Only small lazy ripples broke on the shore with what sounded like a sigh of exhaustion. The glare of the white sky blended with the glitter of the steel-gray sea. Even the tips of the stunted pine by the window were still. The only sounds the grandmother heard in the villa in the early mornings were the faint clucking of the chickens and the sound of the child's high-pitched cries.

Every morning they rose early, before the heat was too great, and sat on the terrace, eating white crumbly bread and drinking bitter coffee, before they traipsed down the daisy-studded stone steps that led like a chain from the terrace to the void of the sea.

The children—the grandmother thought of her son and her

daughter-in-law as children—strolled indolently ahead. The boy
had the long, slender, shapely legs of a tall girl. He carried the
yellow deck chairs under one arm and the newspaper and books
under the other. The girl carried the child casually on one hip
holding her with one arm, absentmindedly, her other hand on
the boy's shoulder before her.

The maid, Speranza, who had come with the villa the grandmother had rented, followed, clutching the large straw picnic
basket with the midday meal against her breast, stopping from
time to time to catch her breath and to listen. She was, apparently, listening to the only sound to be heard, the clucking of the
chickens. The grandmother thought the maid was probably trying to tell, from the sound of the clucking, if the chickens had
laid any eggs.

The grandmother, a thin woman with piercing blue eyes,
brought up the rear, walking even slower and not carrying anything, only holding her hat on her head, the shadow of the
leghorn trembling on her face.

All the time the family was walking down the steps, the
chickens were clucking and Speranza was listening with what
seemed to the grandmother to be hope. Speranza visited the
chickens each morning and evening, looking for any possible
eggs, but the chickens that summer, under the searing beams of
the relentless sun, laid poorly, out of sight, halfway down the
hill, sufficiently far away that the noise and the odor would not
disturb the guests in the rented villa or on the beach.

Still, sometimes, when the grandmother lay restlessly on her
bed in the night, disturbed by dreams or the sounds of the
child's cry, she thought she could smell the stench from the
chickens' cage, which rose in the heat of the night.

.   .   .

The small pebble-stone beach lay at the foot of the hill between rocks. The family stretched out, lined up in a row in the yellow deck chairs. Only Speranza and the baby sat on the stones. Speranza apparently preferred to sit on a towel on the stones with her short legs spread out before her under her full gray skirt.

The grandmother, draped importantly across the deck chair, her hands lying in her lap, watched her daughter-in-law rise and sit on the boy's lap, laying one white limp arm around his neck, playing with the blond curls at the nape of his neck. With their dark-blond heads side by side, close together, their ivory-white skin with its almost blue tinge around the forehead and the eyes, their pale, insouciant gray eyes, the grandmother thought the couple might have been brother and sister. Even their bodies, long-limbed and narrow, their backs arching exaggeratedly, and the veins in the white hands visible, seemed strangely similar. Perhaps, the grandmother thought, they had, somewhere, a common ancestor.

Only the curve of the girl's abdomen showed the faint lines where the skin had stretched, as though her body had been too narrow to carry the weight of the child.

There was about both of them a vague natural carelessness, an unawareness of danger that the grandmother found touching but slightly irritating. The grandmother found the couple's youthfulness, their vulnerability, a little frightening, and at the same time rather boring. The couple made her feel, at fifty, very old. She considered that this sort of amorous display—the girl was now kissing the boy behind one ear—could just as well take place in the privacy of their own bedroom.

She had to admit that she actually preferred her grandchild's or even the maid's company. She really rather preferred the long afternoons in the cool of the kitchen to the sultriness of the mornings, trapped between the rocks, without shade, on the narrow beach. She liked it when the couple rose from the luncheon table, their hands linked, and went to lie down—they seemed to spend an inordinate amount of time lying down under the mosquito net on the mahogany four-poster bed, half-naked, with their books and their newspapers.

Once, the grandmother had inadvertently entered the couple's room. She walked in, raised her eyes to the ceiling, turned and left the room, but not before she had glimpsed the couple, entwined, half-naked, reading their books.

Sometimes the grandmother wondered if that was all they actually did under the mosquito net. She wondered how the baby had come into being at all. The children themselves seemed to share this sentiment, as her daughter-in-law had once said to her, laughing, "All he had to do was to look me in the eye, and I was pregnant."

When the grandmother passed the couple's open window, she often heard the sound of their rather high-pitched voices. They seemed to be talking and laughing, and sometimes, she thought, a little surprised, the girl was singing to the boy.

Whatever it was they did under the mosquito net seemed to take them a great deal of time. They spent most of the afternoon there and retired to bed early at night. After lunch, when they ate in the villa, the children usually left the table before the coffee. The girl would sometimes say something cryptic like, "Got to get back to Septimus," apparently referring to some book, or the boy might say, "Got to find out what's going on in the world," and laugh.

The grandmother would reply, "Oh, go on with you," and wave them away with a lift of her hand, really rather glad to see them go. She found their conversation at table well-meaning but dull. They seemed to her very earnest. They talked about books that she had never read and had no intention of reading. They spoke of Virginia Woolf and Robbe-Grillet. They had even wanted to call the child Virginia, until the grandmother pointed out that Virginia sounded rather like another word, something she had always called her "heart of hearts." In the way of reading, the grandmother herself liked something meaty, something she could get her teeth into, something with a good strong plot and plenty of sex.

But the children spoke with great seriousness of books without plots and of current events, which they followed carefully, exclaiming in horror over certain happenings that shocked them. A lot of things seemed to shock them; they seemed to find a lot of things "beyond the pale"—riots, rapes, thievery and perjury, kidnappings and hijackings. Nothing much, she had to admit, shocked the grandmother anymore; in fact, she had the rather uneasy feeling, at times, that she had done things that would have shocked the children much more, had they known about them, than the events that shocked them.

There was the night she had spent in a hotel with a stranger, a perfect stranger, a man she had met on a train. She had noticed him eyeing her legs—her legs she always felt were her best point—and before she could have said Jack Robinson, there the man was—he was really rather handsome, dark and a little thickset—beside her, with his hand on her heart of hearts. Well, she couldn't help wondering what her son and her daughter-in-law would have thought about that! And she couldn't even say that she regretted it. No, if she was absolutely honest with herself, she didn't really regret anything much in her life, except, perhaps, a few lost opportunities, and there hadn't been many of those.

If the children weren't exclaiming over shocking events (kidnappings or hijackings, thievery and perjury, riots or rapes), they were complimenting each other playfully and calling on the grandmother for her approval, so that the grandmother had the impression she was being called upon to compliment them both.

"She's got the most beautiful eyes, now, doesn't she, Mother? Did you ever see such beautiful gray eyes?" her boy would say, staring at the girl and laughing.

"Of course she does," the grandmother would say, looking from the girl's eyes to the boy's eyes.

Finally, the couple would rise, and the grandmother would sip her black coffee alone and then get up and go out onto the terrace for a while to smoke a cigarette and join Speranza. She would sit in the shadows of the thick walls in the stone-floored kitchen with the child and the maid, sipping iced tea with lemons from the tree in the garden and nibbling the sugary pastries Speranza baked.

The child would often wake early from her nap—for some reason she didn't sleep well that summer—and Speranza would take her to her grandmother. The little girl would sit happily on her grandmother's lap in nothing but an undershirt and pants, glad to have escaped her cot, tugging wordlessly at her grandmother's pearls, until the grandmother, who understood what she wanted, pulled the child's pink toes, one by one, for each of the little piggies and, when the last little piggy ran all the way home, let her hand run up the child's fat leg all the way across the little undershirt to the child's smooth, warm underarm.

If the child was silent, Speranza was never at a loss for words. She talked mainly about food, but sometimes about her past. Like everybody else Speranza had had her love story, or so she told the grandmother over the tea in the kitchen. She told the grandmother of her husband, a man of culture, she said, a musician, a violinist, with what she called a magnificent mustache, who had quite unaccountably gone off, actually jilted her, run away with her hard-earned cash, leaving her to face life alone with her embonpoint and her squint.

As Speranza talked, the child would watch her face as though she could see something interesting happening there. At the time the grandmother thought it was Speranza's squint the child was noticing.

Speranza, sitting now on the beach, knitting, probably dreamed of returning to America with the family and opening a pizza parlor, the grandmother thought. Speranza knitted fast, and sang bits and pieces of a song that sounded, to the grandmother, who sat beside her, something like *"Vado da Lodi a Milano per cercà la mia ginga ging."*

The grandmother watched as the couple rose, picked their way lightly, walking hand in hand across the pebbles, going to the edge of the water, sinking down gently into the sea, reaching out with long languid strokes, swimming until she could hardly see them anymore, turning on their backs, kicking up a rainbow spray in the air.

As they swam back to the shore, the girl called out suddenly from the water to her child, as though she had just remembered her presence. She called over and over again, "Isabelle, belle, Isabelle, IIIsaaaabelllle," until the child's name, with its long-drawn vowel sounds, seemed to fill the beach with a cadence that was both sad and wild. The child, however, ignored her mother's call completely, crouching down in her light blue romper on her little, fat legs, placing the smooth gray stones very carefully one by one into her green bucket.

It was, perhaps, at that moment that the grandmother began

to realize the truth, though afterward she found it hard to say
exactly when it had come to her. Perhaps, she thought, she had
somehow known what would happen from the start.

The grandmother had been against the marriage, though she had
not actually said anything to stop the couple from marrying or at
any rate, had not said as much as her ex-husband had said. Her
ex-husband had said a great deal. He had been dead set against
the match, particularly as the ex-husband himself had been
married four times. He told his son he was too young. He had
not even finished college. He told him that, with all the alimony
he was paying already, he couldn't afford to support yet another
woman, and certainly not his son's wife.

The grandmother had been against the match, but she had
thought it inevitable. After all, there was the child on the way,
and the girl had money of her own, and the couple had, apparently, always been in love.

As long as the grandmother could remember, the girl had
been there, like an omen, she thought sometimes. The couple
had known each other since birth, or almost since birth, had
always been together, or so it seemed to the grandmother. Whenever she turned around to look for her son, that girl was there,
with those slender white arms around his neck, like a weed,
she had thought sometimes, or even a leech. The girl was at
every one of her son's birthday parties, sitting in the flickering
light, watching Charlie Chaplin, one arm flung around the boy's
neck; she went to the same school he did, she followed him to
camp.

There was something about the girl, something delicate,
something hopeless, the grandmother had always thought. She
wasn't sure what it was. Perhaps it was the very white, almost

blue teeth, or the way the girl forgot things, was unable to remember her keys or even the dog, which she left once, for a whole day, howling, tied up at the baker's.

The grandmother had hoped for something better for her boy. But he didn't seem to notice his loss. He had never known anything else.

He was an only child. She should have given him a real sister, perhaps, she thought, not this look-alike, this white shadow, but she had not had the time to make a second child before her husband left her. And perhaps, she thought, it wouldn't have made any difference if she had.

The heat on the beach at noon hung over them ominously. The sky was a glaring void. A vendor came by, bending against the weight of the box on his back, his bare toes splayed on the stones. *"Candit . . . chi vuole?"* he called. No one moved. The girl lay stretched out on the pebbles, resting after her swim, wrapped in a white towel, which she wore drawn up underneath her shoulder, so that her head was cradled on her arm.

Even as the grandmother dozed, her eyes shut on the glare, she was conscious of her daughter-in-law before her and somehow unaccountably perturbed by her still presence.

"I think the treasure is hungry," Speranza said, referring to the child, who was tottering across the pebbles in the general direction of the sea. The maid staggered after the little girl, waving a chicken bone at her.

"Come eat, come eat." Speranza yelled the only two words of English she had learned at the child's back. The child continued, going toward the edge of the water, carrying her green bucket over one arm, gazing out toward the horizon, as though bent on a voyage of discovery.

"Come eat, come eat." Speranza's loud, accented voice filled the beach like a rallying cry.

The grandmother stared at the child and the maid, at the boy and the girl, and it came to the grandmother, then, that what she had suspected all along was perfectly obvious, was there for the whole world to perceive. For a moment, she almost gasped with amazement, not at what she had discovered, but that no one had discovered it before her. What was amazing to her was that no one else had noticed, had been able to notice something so evident. For all these months, the boy and the girl and the child had lived together, day after day and night after night, and never noticed what had become perfectly obvious to the grandmother in the space of a few moments.

The grandmother watched with astonishment as her daughter-in-law rose languidly, with a laugh, and walked on her tiptoes across the stones to pick up the child at the edge of the sea. The mother swung her child around in the air playfully. The girl was actually swinging her child over the water and throwing her head back and laughing, the child's little bare feet rising and falling, rising and falling, rising and falling, skimming the surface of the sea.

The grandmother looked at her son. Her boy was sitting in his deck chair with his straight nose tilted toward the sun, with his perfect profile at the exact angle to obtain the maximum amount of the sun's rays, with his eyes shut and his book spread open on his lap. As for Speranza, she stood with her chicken bone still raised in her hand, probably contemplating the quality of the aspic, the grandmother thought.

The sea and the sky and the pebble-stone beach all looked suddenly gray to the grandmother, as gray as the girl's gray eyes. The sky seemed low and cloudy, and even the smell of the sea, thick and bitter.

As she watched the child fly through the air, she thought that the world would never look quite the same again.

The grandmother had a sudden desire to shout out something obscene; she wanted to say something that would wake everyone up. Instead, she said, "I think it's going to rain," and thought, I'll tell them after lunch.

She waited until dinner. At dinner her son was discussing *The Brothers Karamazov*, or it might have been *War and Peace*. The grandmother was not really listening. Whatever it was, it was long and serious, and not the sort of thing one could easily interrupt. When her son finally paused, and the grandmother was about to broach the subject on her mind, Speranza came in with a huge dish of spaghetti, balanced on the palm of her hand, and launched into a long and detailed description of how to make *ragu*. As Speranza talked, the grandmother thought she had better put the thing off. After all, it was just possible that she might be wrong about the causes, if not the effect. These things were obviously difficult to measure exactly. Perhaps it would be wiser to have a professional opinion, a medical opinion. Perhaps she ought to get a doctor. That was it. Obviously that would be the thing to do. She decided, while Speranza explained the part about letting the red wine simmer, that she would call the doctor the next day, without saying anything to anyone, and have him confirm what she already knew.

The doctor arrived at two the next day, while the couple were napping. He was a slightly stout man with a florid face and wore a dark suit with a linen waistcoat. He mopped his brow, sweating, after his climb up the hill. The grandmother noticed the

slight bulge under his waistcoat and his gold watch. She had a
penchant for chubby men, and she liked the way the thick gold
watch dangled over the swell of his stomach. She stood talking
to him for a moment on the terrace and even offered him a cup
of coffee. He drank the coffee while admiring the view.

The doctor knew the people who lived next door to the villa.

"She's a Dufour, you know," he said, raising his eyebrows
appreciatively.

"Oh really," the grandmother said, as though she did know,
pleased anyway to find herself in such good company.

"And the house on the left belongs to a German, a big in-
dustrialist, you know," the doctor went on, nodding with approval at the view.

The grandmother would have liked to prolong the conversation; she even considered, for one mad moment, putting the
whole thing off and throwing an elegant dinner party for her
neighbors and the doctor. She saw herself in her best blue dress,
coming out onto the candlelit terrace, followed by Speranza with
a silver dish of canapés.

Instead, she ushered the doctor through the French doors that
led from the terrace into the child's room.

The child's room was dimly lit, the curtains closed on the
heat of the afternoon. There was a faint odor of urine in the air.
The little girl was standing up in nothing but her diaper, in her
crib. She was bouncing, rocking herself back and forth against
the bars of the crib, so that it had moved halfway across
the floor.

When the child saw the grandmother, she lifted her arms to
her. The grandmother picked up the child and put her down by

the window, giving her her box of blocks and drawing back the curtains to let the light into the room.

While the child piled the blocks into a neat tower, the doctor clapped his hands loudly behind her back.

The child went on making her tower.

The doctor moved a little closer and clapped again.

The child carefully balanced the last tiny block on the top of the tower.

The grandmother looked at the doctor inquiringly.

"Of course these things are difficult to assess with a young child," the doctor said, and mopped his brow. He cleared his throat and added, "They can do wonderful things these days. You would be amazed at what they can do. They can practically build you a new ear these days. And in America, I'm sure, they can do miracles. In America they're always coming up with something new. Why, who knows what they might be inventing even at this very moment. Of course, now, if it should be . . ."

At that point the couple came into the doorway. They stood on the threshold of the small room, the boy leaning against the jamb, the girl leaning against the boy, one arm around his waist. The boy wore his shorts cut off at the knee and an undershirt, and the girl, a sleeveless cotton dress. You could see her pink knees. Neither of the children had brushed their hair, and their faces were creased with sleep. For a moment they stood there in silence.

In the garden halfway down the hill, the chickens clucked in the heat, and the cicadas shrilled.

"What's going on?" the boy said eventually, shaking his head, looking from the doctor to the child, who sat on the floor with the tower of brightly colored blocks before her.

The girl went over to pick up the child, sweeping her from the floor fast, as though she were in danger of some sort. As she swept the child up, she inadvertently knocked over the tower of blocks. The child began to wail. The girl clutched her child to her chest.

The grandmother looked at the doctor, who wiped his face with his handkerchief.

"I don't think that child can hear," the grandmother said in a clear voice over Isabelle's screams.

The girl looked at the grandmother as though she had insulted her personally. She drew herself up. "What are you talking about? What is the doctor doing here? Why did you call the doctor without telling us? How could you call the doctor without even asking our opinion? Isabelle is not ill," the girl said, hugging the child to her breast protectively, jiggling the screaming child up and down fast.

The doctor looked embarrassed. He glanced at the grandmother and then at the couple, and murmured something vague: "*Una bella bambina*, a beautiful child, not so? Perhaps, eventually, a checkup, when you get her back home, just to make sure all is perfectly well. Just a routine checkup to make sure everything's in order. Very difficult to say anything at such a young age." Then he looked at the gold watch on his chest and added, "I have an appointment. I'm afraid I'll have to be going," and he hurried out of the room through the French doors onto the terrace.

Everyone followed the doctor out onto the terrace. Even Speranza, in her best lace cap, had made an appearance by then, drawn by the sounds of drama. The doctor shook hands hastily all around, bowed and murmured something no one could catch through the child's cries.

As the doctor walked down the stone steps to the road, he

called out over his shoulder, waving his plump hand in the air. "They can do wonderful things these days, you know. In America they can do wonderful things; they can do miracles in America," he called as he descended the daisy-studded stone steps that led like a chain through the garden.

The grandmother hurried after the doctor, calling to him, suddenly remembering that she had not paid the man. At first he told her the visit had cost nothing, nothing at all, bowing and mopping his forehead at the same time. The grandmother insisted, pulling the large Italian bills out of her handbag. As she pulled the lire from her purse, a slight breeze blew up the hill, and the stench of the chickens in their cage came to her. She shook the doctor's damp hand again and thanked him and walked slowly back up the steep steps. Really, she thought, with what they charged for a month in the villa, they could have removed their chickens.

She heard Speranza say, "What does everybody want for dinner tonight?"

"Spaghetti," both the children called out at once, joyfully. "We want spaghetti," they said, and laughed.

THE APARTMENT

She was complaining about the dearth of possibilities, as did everyone else in that place, saying something vague about the difficulty of finding anything in any way suitable, when she became aware of him moving toward her on the terrace. She did not actually see him approach but felt his presence, as one feels a draft of air and looks up to see if someone has opened a window or a door. But she was already out of doors. Afterward she would not remember whose terrace it was or even to whom she had been speaking, or why she happened to have been there at the party that night.

Since her arrival in the city—she had come here to read a paper on her research—she had not often attended parties. The paper had been well received, and they had asked her to stay on, finding her a small dreary place with a depressing view of a wall. Her days were all the same. She spent them working. At night she came home late, walking fast through the shadowed streets with their odor of decay, bolting her door behind her twice, and pouring a double whiskey as soon as she had entered her place, slumping down in front of the television with whatever she could find in the refrigerator, watching, half-dazed, the flickering images until she was no longer able to watch, and then dragging herself into the closet-sized bedroom and sinking down onto the mattress on the floor, falling immediately into a heavy dreamless sleep.

She had the impression that she had been standing with her back to the wall, situated where she could see the city glittering below and yet remain near enough the source of ice that had been put out by her host.

Or was it hostess?

To whomever the apartment belonged, it was a grand establishment: a seemingly endless, brightly lit space, with mirrored walls, a thousand shifting reflections caught in glass, immense windows opening onto the terrace and the city. Between the windows and the mirrors hung eighteenth-century paintings.

Where exactly the man had come from, through a side door from an adjoining room or, unnoticed, through one of the sliding windows from the living room, it was impossible for her to tell.

What struck her immediately about the man was his eyes. It seemed to her as if the fellow was taking in every detail of her appearance. He stared at her out of pale, slightly protuberant red-lashed eyes. Perhaps it was the effect of the alcohol she had drunk, but seeing the man standing there with his eyes on her, the woman thought the man had something rather too forceful about him. His hair was parted in the middle of a shiny forehead with a curl on either side, and he wore something theatrical in black or anyway in midnight blue, and there might have been (though surely she was mistaken) a pince-nez around the fellow's neck. At any rate he was quite obviously a foreigner.

Speaking in a low voice with a slight accent she was as yet unable to place, the man said, "I might be able to help you."

Drawing herself up, she said, "I'm not actually looking right now. The university has provided something quite satisfactory."

"Ah," the man went on in a low, thick, slightly amused voice, his hand hovering somewhere near her shoulder, leading her away from the wall, toward the edge of the terrace, "but once you've caught a glimpse of this, you will not settle for anything else."

The accent, she thought then, was most certainly Slavonic.
"It's very large, very open," he went on.

She said, almost in a whisper, "Open?"

"Oh, yes," the man said, opening his arms to the city, to the
deep blue of the summer sky and to the hum of the traffic that
came up to them with what seemed to her a sound like the sea.

She noticed that his sleeves seemed too short for his arms,
and that the backs of his hands were smooth and spotted with
age. She moved a little closer to him, so that her arm almost
brushed his sleeve. Leaning against the railing, suddenly giddy,
she found herself saying, "How much would you say it was?"

The man mentioned a sum. All she could do was raise her
handkerchief to her brow and repeat the amount. He laughed,
curling back his lips to lay bare long, slightly yellow teeth.
There was nothing contagious about his hilarity. When the man
had stopped laughing, he whispered something.

"What was that?" she asked, turning toward him.

The man was still whispering something about the previous
tenant, who had been quite unacceptable and who had left
somewhat unexpectedly. As he said this—or whatever it was he
was saying—his hand, which had been resting on the railing,
darted toward her and dived inside the round collar of her dress,
slid down and clamped itself around her breast. The lights of the
city seemed to swing around her. She closed her eyes for a
moment.

When she looked up, the man had gone.

She knew from her work that certain snake venoms kill by
working on the blood: the cells are made to burst, coagulation is
impeded, and the animal hemorrhages to death. Other venoms

break up the impulses running to the heart; it begins to beat wildly for a moment and then ceases altogether. Still other venoms attack the nerves: the motor functions are interrupted, paralysis sets in, respiration stops.

It was the ones that attack the nerves that interested her most. She was particularly interested in the idea that the same venom that paralyzes the nerves could stimulate their growth. It was not a novel idea, she realized; since medieval times, and probably before, toxins had been used as remedies. But it was an idea that had not been, to her mind, fully exploited. She recalled the line: *In poison there is physic.*

She went to bed late and no doubt more than a little inebriated, stumbling into her room. Lying on her dusty mattress, she was unable to sleep. For some reason, perhaps the heat or her somewhat unsteady state, the man's words kept coming back to her. In a series of images so vivid they had the effect of hallucinations, she saw triple-arched casements of stained glass giving onto gardens bright with exotic bloom and tropical trees beneath a brilliant sky; pale gardenias mingling with plumbago, feathery acacias spreading wide trembling shadows on the tall grass; royal palms, their long trunks covered over with clinging vines, rising from beds of lush greenery into the steamy air; fountains, whose swift flow caught the light and shimmered in the colors of the rainbow, soaring high from deep pools of still water; and, hanging from the twisted branches and creeping vines of the strange, dreamlike trees, green and black mambas coiling, blinking jewel-like eyes.

She had never liked Sundays. She sat up with difficulty and smoked several cigarettes before dragging herself from the mattress and making her way into the kitchen, her eyes still half-closed.

At first she did not notice what lay on the floor by the door. Even when she did notice it, she hesitated, drew her robe tightly about her, staring a while into the fluorescent emptiness of the refrigerator before bending to pick it up. She did not immediately open the envelope but put it aside, fried two eggs, extracted a cup from the dishes in the sink, boiled water for coffee, and then settled herself before the television, glancing down from time to time at the rather formal lettering. Finally she got to her feet, took a few steps into the room, and stared at the miscellany of furniture—things, she supposed, abandoned by visiting professors or perhaps bought hastily to fill in a gap: the two straw armchairs with their loose cushions, the backless sofa, the painted cupboard with its spotted unreflecting mirror, the dead geranium strangled in its rock-dry soil, and her books in dusty scattered piles on the floor. The rest of her things were still in cardboard boxes. She stood idly, her back to the door, smoking cigarette after cigarette before the grimy window, looking across at the brick wall and the windows with the lowered shades. She imagined people moving with purpose behind the shades: perhaps women with glazed eyes holding drooling infants lifted against their shoulders, or men shaving before bathroom mirrors, drawing careful blades over smooth soapy skin, or couples touching between rumpled sticky sheets, or children turning the leaves of picture books, dreaming.

She supposed that middle-aged female scientists of respectable reputation, smelling slightly of smoke and formaldehyde, with visible collarbones, chalky skins, pallid green eyes, and what appeared to her to be, when she stared at herself in the bathroom mirror in the early-morning light, some sort of mel-

ancholic self-abnegation in the lines around the mouth, were not
in great demand. Besides, she felt that she labored always on
the edge of exhaustion, her life dedicated to what she considered
a rigid and demanding service, contriving only through prodi-
gious spasms of will to produce work that had brought her some
measure of acclaim.

She opened the envelope and held the sheet of blue paper in
her hands. She glanced down at the signature. It appeared to her
to be a rather too complicated name. She moved over to the sofa,
sank down onto the cushions, and let the letter lie in her lap.

She was unable to find the listing for the name given with the
address in the letter. If she wanted to see the place, she supposed, she would have to go in person. It was late afternoon by
the time she had prepared herself, pinning up her fair hair
carefully at the nape of her neck. She decided that her attire, a
black linen dress with white gloves, white shoes, and white
purse, was sufficiently respectable. Not that she saw anyone
noticing her attire when she stepped out into the trapped heat,
standing on melting tar, shading her face from the glare of the
light, and shrinking back from the rank odor of the steamy
narrow street. This part of the city was dead quiet. She found a
taxi immediately, almost as though, she thought, the battered
vehicle that came creeping along the curb had been waiting for
her approach. When she gave the driver the address, he glanced
back at her with what seemed a knowing smile and then took off
with a screech of tires. She leaned back against the worn plastic
seat, opened the window, let the air fan her cheek, and closed
her eyes for a moment. She was tired from her disturbed sleep
of the night before, from the heat, from the motion of the car.

She thought she heard the driver complaining of the heat, the pollution, the filth of the city. She had the sudden impression of his not being a taxi driver at all but some sort of criminal. Rousing herself and glancing at the meter she realized they must have covered a considerable distance. She took off her gloves, kicked off her shoes, sat forward on her seat. She watched the meter closely, took money from her purse, counted it out in readiness.

They were in a part of the city she had never been in before. Despite the twilight the metal of the car turned the small space into a furnace. She rolled down both windows and hung halfway out. The sooty air blew into her hair, settling in it like fine ashes. Her dress clung to her back, soaked with perspiration. All the streets looked the same, stretching before her in the haze.

"There!" As soon as she spotted the name she lurched forward and told the driver, "There. That street there!" The meter had already run up a considerable sum. She paid and saw the driver pull the cab away from the curb without even counting what she had given him.

The dead-end cobblestone street curved slightly, going toward the river, flanked on either side by tall trees, probably some kind of acacia, their feathery leaves fluttering slightly, their shadows moving on the rutted street. An unusual display of flowers and climbing plants grew in the window boxes of the dark housefronts. She walked along the street slowly, hesitating, suddenly conscious of her disarray: her soiled gloves, her wrinkled dress, the unbuttoned waist. Even her shoes were scuffed from the bruising of the cobblestones.

She made out the number of the building she was hunting for, a long gabled front of red brick that arched against the sky and seemed to her, almost, to hang in midair, its shadow at her feet. She stood, leaning back, her thin heels digging into the spaces between the stones, looking at the thick ivy laid over the facade.

She climbed the steps and found herself in a gloomy vestibule. She pressed one and then another of the unnamed but well-polished bells. She fumbled in her handbag to find the letter. She heard a door open and footsteps in the hall. A young man was looking down at her, his blond hair tied back from his neck with a black ribbon. He wore an undershirt and jeans, and had an earring suspended from one ear.

He carried a thick bunch of keys at his belt, and in his hand was a duster. He hovered there, caressing the two shining bells with the duster and showing a row of bluish, almost transparent teeth in a fixed smile.

She could not find the letter in her handbag and was attempting to explain her presence when the man cut her short, saying, as though he had been expecting her, that she would have to wait. His skin glistened with what she thought was either an unhealthy pallor or simply the effect of the half-light of the corridor, as he walked away, swinging his narrow hips ever so slightly.

When he came back he led her up the stairs into a vast empty room that occupied the entire floor. It was cold, quiet, and almost entirely enclosed in glass. Glass sliding doors opened onto a terrace on both sides and a skylight opened above her, so that looking up, she had the fragmented light in her eyes. Beyond back gardens, where trees—or rather the overgrown sumacs that passed for trees in that city—grew, she could see as far as the river, which, caught in the light of the westering sun, shone smoothly.

She surveyed the ample white kitchen and the mirrored bathroom and walked across the polished parquet floor to a bowl of faded lilies. She leaned close to draw in their heavy perfume.

She swung open the built-in closets that covered a wall. A man's black jacket hung at one end. She ran her fingers over the hand stitching on the silk of the lapels, plunged her hands into the empty pockets, and came up with a coin, which she placed in her pocket. Then she slipped into the jacket. It fit her almost perfectly, she realized, standing before the mirror, turning left, then right. Whoever had owned the jacket had been of narrow build.

When the super, if indeed he was a super, returned, she was still wearing the jacket, looking out over the back garden. Turning to the man and lifting the lapel of the jacket, she asked, "What happened to him?"

The man stared down at the garden below. He said, "I don't think you need worry about him."

"Not worry?" she asked.

The fellow said, "He's not likely to come back."

"You mean he could come back?" she asked.

"In theory only," the man said, adding, "They've put him wherever they put them—you know?"

"Is he—?" She tapped her forehead.

He said, "Oh, not that, not that at all. If you're interested, you'd better leave a deposit. At this price the thing'll be snapped up fast. Whatever you have will do nicely. We can settle the rest later."

The transaction was made over the mantelpiece. As she leaned toward him to hand him the money, she was suddenly aware of what looked to her like a birthmark on the back of his arm and at the same time a strange odor that reminded her of nothing so much as the odor of a hospital.

That week her work progressed. She was filled with a most surprising sense of what seemed to her a lowering of inward barriers, a new freedom, a consciousness of the infinite power of the mind, something she recollected feeling in moments of youthful ardor, something so new, or at any rate so long outgrown, that it surprised her.

Her work, she realized, was still very much in its initial stages; the marvels of the new uses of the snake venom came to her only in a series of images. She saw the dying nerve cells, stimulated by the venom, springing to life.

The young man received her, this time, in what appeared to be his room in the basement of the building. The place seemed to her dark and stuffy, the window apparently hermetically closed. Drawn across the middle of the room was a red curtain behind which, she supposed, there would be a bed.

The man offered her some wine. He sat by her side on the shabby plastic sofa, crossing his long legs at the ankle, while she sipped. He asked her if she still wanted it.

"Well, yes, if it can be done without any hitch," she said.

"Of course, there have been other applicants, as you can imagine, with a place like this," he said, filling her glass again.

She asked, "Has an agreement already been made with someone else?"

"I doubt it. As far as I'm concerned, you'd be the most suitable."

"Suitable?" she asked.

"Well yes, you know—single woman. You are single, aren't you?"

"Oh yes, I'm single," she replied.

He asked, staring at her directly, "Never married?"

Adjusting the folds of her skirt and looking down at her lap, she said, "No."

"And no family, no ties? Am I right?" he asked.

"Nothing to speak of," she said.

"And, I'm sure responsible and"—he seemed to cast about an instant and then continued, shuffling papers before him on his knee—"not too young."

She laughed and drew back slightly. "What about the lease?" she asked.

"Oh there's no problem as far as that goes. Only a slight formality," he said.

At length she asked, "What is this formality?" picking at a hole in the arm of the sofa.

"You see, I would like the lease to remain within the family, so to speak," he said.

She asked him, "Whose family?"

"Well, as a matter of fact, my family, or rather my name. I would like to keep the lease in the same name," he said.

Trying to concentrate, she asked, "The same name? If the lease is in your name why don't you live in the apartment?"

"Legally, the lease could remain in the same name," he said quickly. "Only a formality of course, a piece of paper, a *mariage blanc*, naturally," he said, with what seemed to her like serenity.

She rose, looked at her watch, exclaimed at the lateness of the hour. She would have to leave, indeed she would have to leave immediately, adding as she weaved her way toward the door that she would think it over.

In the taxi going home she leaned back against the seat, shut her eyes, and let the air blow on her face. She felt slightly nauseated. After a while, she closed the window on the odor of the rotting streets.

She continued to work long hours, but she had difficulty getting out of bed in the mornings and sometimes remained somnolent, coiled lazily on her mattress in the dusty sunlight. She hoped she was not ill. She made little effort to clean her apartment and let the dust lie. She stacked her books up in piles but otherwise did not arrange the furniture. From time to time she thought of plans for a more active social life, but she did nothing.

One evening, coming home on a bus, she stood in the crowded aisle. Behind her she could feel a man's body pressed against hers, the pressure gradually growing. She held herself erect, tense, leaning as much as possible toward the door, her eyes fixed on the advertisement over the door, words she did not comprehend. The old vehicle rattled and rocked; the wheels screeched. The man's pelvis pressed up against her, rocking back and forth with the movement of the bus. She let herself sink back into the warmth of the man's flesh. She felt him lift her skirt from behind, his hand slithering up her thigh, caressing her slowly, his fingers craftily probing, finding their way to the heart of her heat.

When the bus stopped, she stepped out and turned her head

for a moment. He was already disappearing into the crowd, but the neat curl of blond hair and the black ribbon were unmistakable.

She walked the rest of the way home, stumbling along, her eyes on the sidewalk, her body trembling. As she walked, the thought that came to her suddenly was: *It doesn't mean anything. What difference will it make, now, at my age, after all. It will make no difference at all. I will go on working as before. After all,* Paris vaut une messe.

Two months after the move to her new place, with her new name, her article on her subject appeared in a scientific journal and received a certain acclaim from prominent scientists in her field. Her position at the university was secured and improved. She was sought out, her opinion listened to, her advice on new projects required. She was asked to lecture in various institutions of note. Rumors of her success circulated. She was criticized, of course, in secret. It was said she had gone too far. Old friends suddenly resurfaced. New friends called. She was entertained. She decided that she, too, would entertain. She would give a party. She would hold a housewarming in her new place. She bought new furniture: modern chairs in leather with clean spare lines, a large thick glass table with steel legs, Kilim carpets of some value in blues and reds, an abstract painting that she hung over the mantelpiece. She bought a dazzling silk evening dress that clung to her body.

The day of the party, she placed large bowls of freesias, red roses, and arum lilies at both ends of the big room so that their perfume filled the air. She spread white platters of brightly colored raw vegetables, cheeses, sliced hams and sausages, long fresh loaves of brown and white bread across the glass-topped table. She baked apple pies and kept them warm to serve with whipped cream.

She stood in the bathroom in her pink silk slip. She smoothed a dark foundation on her pale skin and brushed her cheeks with a terra cotta blush. She plucked her eyebrows into fine lines and outlined them with dark pencil. She applied a shiny eye makeup thickly to her lids so that they glittered brightly. She drew a moist red lipstick over her mouth, adding to the slight curve of her lips. She brushed out her hair, slowly drawing the brush with a slight crackle through the fine strands until they shone. She let her hair fall in motionless curls along the line of her neck. Finally she stepped into her dress, moving her hips slightly from side to side with a sinuous movement.

She went about her place slowly, adjusting ashtrays, cushions, and a stray bloom that had fallen to the floor. She left the front door open and stood there, greeting the stream of guests who seemed to arrive all together in a rush.

As for the man whose name she shared, he appeared to have left the city. She presumed he had left for some cooler place. Perhaps, the thought occurred to her, he might be ill, seriously ill. Since her move to her new place she had never seen him on the stairs or in the vestibule. He had never knocked on her door. Gradually, she had almost come to forget him.

Suddenly she noticed the man she had met on the terrace coming through the crowd. She was not surprised. Blinking red lashes over pale, slightly protuberant eyes, he excused himself for crashing the gate. "Well, and how do you like it?" he asked.

"It's a wonderful place," she said, her voice sounding strange in her ears.

He said, "*You* look wonderful," and added in a theatrical whisper, "Apparently marriage becomes you." He looked her up and down slowly.

She felt as though she were watching herself from afar, or rather watching a stranger standing there in a clinging, shiny dress, someone much younger than she was who might, quite absurdly, break into a Middle Eastern dance, rolling her hips and swinging her arms.

He said, "Was I right?"

"Oh yes, from the moment I saw it," she said and added, after a pause, "I ought to have thanked you in some way."

"You already have. You must let me and my friend take you out to dinner one night. I know just the place," he said.

"I'm sure you do," she said.

The place he chose seemed to her to be hardly suitable initially. It was dark and hot. Each table was lit with a small lamp that cast a circle of reddish light on the ceiling.

She sat trapped in a corner between the younger and the older one. The younger one, who had suddenly reappeared on the stairs with his duster just after her party, looked somewhat recovered, she thought, at any rate temporarily, from his illness, if he had indeed been ill. He had put on some weight, and his cheeks shone, though the reddish sheen of the skin might have been induced, she thought, by some artificial means.

The older one, in black, smiled his half-smile. He leaned across the table, lifting his frosted glass to theirs, gazing first at the younger man and then at her, and saying, "To both of you, may your union be prosperous and bring forth fruit," swallowing down the vodka fast.

When she hesitated to drink, he insisted that she knock it back. She did.

While she struggled with the food, she attempted to concentrate on what the younger one said. He now held forth with the apparently unquestioning assumption of his marital prerogatives. He was once again employed. He was earning a large salary.

She was not listening.

She was beginning to comprehend.

THE TOKOLOSH

The native boy has a name for the child. He calls her Sk. Sk. Skatie for the S. and the K. on the christening bowl. The name the native gives her is nothing to her. She does not care to be called Sk.Sk.Skatie, with a laugh and a grin as though, she thinks, the name itself were a joke she has never understood, or even that she herself were a joke she has never understood. She has her own lovely name that her mother has given her. She does not like to hear the native boy call out Sk.Sk.Skatie, lifting his head from his polishing and laughing as she walks by with the red hibiscus in her thick blond hair, going out to play doll in the garden. "Don't you dare call me that," she says. "If you call me that again I'll tell Mummy to punish you for calling me that, for being a cheeky native boy." She has a perfectly good name, and he is to call her by that name.

The native boy goes on calling her the name he has given her, and when she tells her mother about it, her mother only smiles and shrugs her white shoulders and lets her small beringed hands flutter up to her hair and down into her lap.

There are times, however, when the native boy does not call the child by the name he has given the child, when he does not call her by the name her mother gave her, does not call her anything at all.

Now the heavy luncheon, the luncheon with the roast beef and the two green vegetables and the Yorkshire pudding and the potatoes, which the native boy serves with his pink-palmed black hands on oven-hot willow-pattern plates, begins. The native boy stands by the sideboard in his white starched serving suit with the blue band, the band that goes from his shoulder to his waist and has a little tassel that sways back and forth. He taps with the opener against the bottles on the sideboard until the child turns her head. She tells him which of the bottles, the ginger ale or the ginger beer or the lemon squash, she wishes to drink. The mother and the nanny go on drinking wine mixed with a little soda water, the pomegranate-colored liquid sparkling in a cut-glass pitcher. His white starched serving suit rustles and the blue tassel sways back and forth each time he reaches across the table to fill the empty glasses.

The mother leans toward the nanny and whispers something, raising her thin dark eyebrows high, her hazel eyes bright.

The nanny shakes her head slowly from side to side, keeping her gaze fixed before her on the stiff flowers in the center of the table. The nanny turns her head slowly and clucks her tongue and says, "Good heavens," and then even though the nanny has told the child never to take the Lord's name in vain, "My God," and then, glancing at the child, "Little pitchers have big ears."

The mother sips her wine and says, "It makes me shiver to think of it. Out there in that desolate place. They found her in nothing but a pink petticoat."

The nanny's eyes bulge and blink and her nose sticks out like a beak. She says, "I don't know that I'll ever get used to this country. The violence."

The mother says, "Suffocated, my dear. Can you imagine!"

The nanny shivers too. She sighs and looks out the window and clasps her hands and says, "How I long for a hedgerow. How I long for the little lambs in the spring. My skin is drying up in all this sun."

The mother says, "My father used to say women don't do well out here," and nods to the native boy to fill her glass again, lifting up the cut-glass beaker in the air.

The mother says to him, "Close the curtains, could you. The light is beginning to give me a migraine," and lifts one hand to rearrange the waves of her dark hair. The child watches the light gleam in the hollows of the lustrous curls.

While the nanny and the mother have their coffee and crème de menthe on the glassed veranda, sitting in wicker chairs and staring out at the dun grass, murmuring in low voices, the child stands with her back to the sink, watching the native boy, who is polishing the silver. She likes to see him laying out the sheets of newspaper across the kitchen table, the crumpled newspaper that flutters and crackles, and to see him polishing the silver with a small toothbrush, over and over until the initials on the christening bowl are so faint she can hardly see them anymore.

Then the nanny in her white uniform and her white shoes is standing at the door of the kitchen and calling the child for her nap, the nap the child takes every afternoon, that stretches from almost immediately after the heavy luncheon until the long shadows of the big house cover the grass. The nanny tells the child that if she will come right away without any fuss, nanny will let her stroke her sticky double chins.

The child hangs back, holding the nanny's hand but looking back for a moment over her shoulder to see what the native boy is doing, to see if he is still polishing. Perhaps she looks back because she sometimes suspects that when she is not looking, the native boy does not polish the silver or the floors or the string of shiny cars or the shoes or even the soles of the shoes, but when she is no longer looking, his long thin black body grows longer and thinner, grows to be as long and thin and black as nothing but a shadow on a wall, and then the native boy turns himself into the tokolosh, the evil spirit that the native boy says hides down in the water at the bottom of the garden beyond the stile.

The child walks slowly along the corridor staring up at the Cries of London that line the wall. She goes into the nursery and does as she is told to hurry up and do: she takes off the little socks and the little red shoes and folds the dress and lies down on her bed in her vest and pants in the big half-darkened nursery under the mosquito net. She listens to the nanny's stertorous breathing and the crickets rasping, not thinking about the native boy who is nothing but a shadow to her, but thinking about the mother who is downstairs in the lounge, the child thinks, embroidering. She thinks of the tablecloth with the red hibiscus pattern that spreads like a stain across the center of the cloth so slowly that the child imagines the mother must undo what she has just done each day. The child thinks of the lovely red petals growing in the lounge below. She thinks of the stillness of the lounge, of the fireplaces at each end that seem to her to gape like empty mouths, and of the grandfather clock that the man comes once a week to wind with a little key, and of the big bowl of gray proteas that look to the child to be almost dead.

Now she rises slowly and descends the steps. The house is very quiet in the early afternoon. She tries to open the door to the lounge, but the door is locked. The kitchen door, too, is shut now, and she thinks the native boy must be eating his mealie pap with his fingers at the wooden table in the yard, or lying on the bed briefly in his tiny windowless room, smoking *dagga*, which the nanny has told the child is something that makes the natives go mad.

But the native boy is not in his room or in the yard; the native boy is crouching down with his back against the brick wall, outside the kitchen, smoking his pipe in the sun. The child tells him to come and help her ride her new bicycle. She tells him to hold her on the bicycle so that she does not fall. He runs beside her with his damp hands on her back and on the handle-bars of the new bicycle, pushing her forward, shouting "Gaashly, Skatie, gaashly," running beside her panting, his toes thrust through the holes in his white tennis shoes. The ground slopes slightly and the coarse kikuyu grass cushions the wheels of her bicycle. "Let me go, let me go," she says. He lets go. She begins to gather speed. He laughs at her and claps his hands and stamps his feet rhythmically against the earth, bending his knees with his back straight, bringing his feet down firmly, pounding the ground. Then he lifts one foot and then the other and throws them forward toward her.

She is flying now with the wind on her face, the ground dipping away from her.

"Stop, stop, Skatie," the native boy yells from the bank, waving a dishcloth in the air. But she is going toward the banana tree, going straight down the hill toward the banana tree.

When she opens her eyes the native boy is carrying her across the lawn. She is breathing in his odor of sweat and tobacco and dried leaves. He is singing her his song.

That night she wakes with a light shining in the nursery window. She does not know why the light shines on her bed or why the light frightens her. She thinks she hears something downstairs in the lounge. She slips silently from her bed and runs along the corridor with the Cries of London prints to her mother's bedroom, finding the door open to her. But her mother is not propped up on the white pillows as she is in the mornings. Her mother does not turn to the child, as she does in the mornings, reaching out both white arms, letting the child climb up under the linen sheets and the pink silk eiderdown, loosening the lace of her gown and letting the child suck upon her slack breast.

The child goes down the green-carpeted stairs.

The door to the lounge is ajar. The child stands on the threshold of the big room at the top of the steps that lead down into the lounge. At first the child thinks there is no one else in the dimly lit room. She looks for the mother and the embroidery, but she sees only the gaping mouths of the fireplaces, the grandfather clock, and the big bowl of gray proteas. She is quite sure there is no one sitting in the armchair by the fireplace, no one on the sofa, no one even on the piano stool, where her mother sometimes sits, not playing the piano but just sitting there with her glass on the piano and her hands hovering over the keys like moths.

The child steps quietly down into the room, her bare toes sinking into the thick pile of the carpet, listening to the ticking of the grandfather clock and the continuous rasping of the crickets in the garden and to some other unfamiliar sound that she thinks might be the heavy breathing of some creature. Now she can no longer move, though the shaking of her body, she thinks, must move the floor beneath her.

She stands quite still.

In the shadows, stretched out on the floor near the open mouth of the fireplace, she can see something that seems to move very slightly and groan or make a noise that sounds to her like a groan. She draws a little closer, and it is then that the small beringed hands reach up and draw her down, down. She tries to draw back, but her hand is caught. Something is drawing her down onto the carpet with the pomegranate pattern, something is drawing her down and under, something is sucking on her mouth. In the half-light she cannot see the thing's face, but whatever it is holds on to the child tightly, and she cannot free herself. She tries to pull away from it, but it clings to her with its hot grasping hands and draws her closer to its hot stinking breath. It slumps forward heavily, falling onto its knees, dragging her down onto the carpet, dragging her down beside it, under it, fastening its wet stinking mouth onto hers, sucking at her. She is locked to it, caught up in its flesh.

She is screaming and screaming.

Now the native boy is there. He lifts the thing from her, loosens its small white hands and, very gently, lifts it across one shoulder, takes it on his long thin back. He turns and walks up the steps out of the lounge. The child thinks the native boy will take it out into the garden and dump it in the compost heap, but instead the boy goes on up the stairs with it. The child stands at the bottom of the stairs and watches the small white hands that swing back and forth, banging against the boy's back.

MY BOY'S GIRL

I've got to get this off my chest. I want you to know that I have never been able to do much with my boy. Even when he was quite a small child, I couldn't do much with him; I could never even catch him to spank him. He could always run faster than I, so you can imagine what it was like later on. He's the wall type, if you know what I mean: stubborn. Besides, if you think about it, who of us has been able to do anything with our children?

Now, where to start? I suppose with the Italian. The Italian will do as well as anything. I suppose you could say, arbitrarily, of course, that the thing started, as so many things have, with the Italian.

There was a soft breeze from the sea the day the Italian arrived in the rooms we rented on the top floor of that house. The rooms had a terrace on the garden side and not facing the sea. They had wicker furniture and faded cretonne curtains, paper-thin walls and slippery tiled floors that shook a little and squeaked as you walked, the sand from the beach gritty beneath your feet. We took the rooms because of the garden and because of the price. My alimony, you know, comes in dollars, and the dollar just then was rather weak. As it turned out, the landlord never gave us the key to the iron gate of the closed garden, and we could only stand, enviously, looking down into the well of shiny tropical plants and lush green shade with the scent of magnolias rising up to us on our terrace in the heat.

A charming boy, the Italian, I thought, with his black hair brushed neatly back from his high forehead, his white linen suit, his elaborate manners, and a leather-bound book in his hand. We sat on the terrace sipping cool drinks at dusk, the boy's pale forehead glimmering in the half-light. I asked questions. I'm good at that. He and my boy talked.

What the Italian talked about was the girl he had met by chance in Rome. He said the girl owned diamond mines, so many diamond mines, and shook out his long white fingers from the wrist, like money, it seemed to me, falling from trees. He was not sure what the girl was actually doing in Rome, or what had brought her and her family to the Eternal City from their lonely home in some vast wilderness. The Italian said the family had a furnished apartment in Rome with a Watteau clown in white, a table with magnificent butterflies in phosphorescent blues and blacks pressed under glass, and a maid who spoke no known language, and who followed the girl like a shadow wherever she walked. He said the girl studied Italian with a private tutor, crossing the river to go to the tutor's small shuttered flat, where the tutor sat intoning Dante, fervently, tears in her eyes, a hand on her bosom, a dark shadow on her top lip.

As the Italian was talking, I watched him fingering the leaves of the leather-bound volume, a gift he told us, from the girl, something old and quite unreadable, I thought, Corneille, or perhaps it was Racine. I watched as the Italian turned the fine pages of the book, and the breeze blew, stirring the scent of magnolia, wafting a photograph to the dusty floor.

The boys bent to pick up the photograph, knocking heads, the dark against the blond. I noticed that it was my boy who clasped the photograph in his hand and lifted it up to the fading light.

My boy said, "Not bad," shrugging his shoulders with apparent nonchalance and then handing it over to me.

I said, "Quite pretty, indeed," and nodded appreciatively at the Italian. What else could I do?

Now I want you to know that before my boy left for Rome, I said to him, lifting an ancient Chinese vase, a gift from a lover— there have been a few of those—into the air, "If you steal that boy's girl, I'll break this over your head." We laughed, and of course my boy set out to do exactly that. As I said, there was never much I could do with him.

What happened in Rome, I can only surmise. This is how I see it: the Italian is standing in the shadows of some baroque church, elegantly waving his fingers at a dark painting. He speaks volubly, offering up what he has: his ancient city, his cultivation, his love of art. The Italian says, "Look at the line of that shoulder. How it flows."

I see the girl beside the Italian in a white dress with a high collar and a billowy skirt. Her cheeks are tinged with carmine. Her transparent eyes wander from the line of the Madonna's shoulder to the window above. She watches a swallow drift like a windblown leaf across the sky. Or perhaps she stares at a beam of light on the stone floor. She does not look at my boy, who stands near her, long and loose-limbed, his white shirt sleeves turned back to the bony elbows. He gazes avidly at the girl, taking in the long neck and the swell of the breasts.

I can only presume that the glances had little or no effect, for the girl departed one night, went off wordlessly with the mother and the aunt, drifted north, so my boy said. Who knows why? Perhaps the girl went north for the music, for the vista from the castle, which is, they say, splendid, or perhaps for want of anything better to do.

What happened next my boy described to me over the telephone. He told me how he had followed the girl in hot pursuit, driving all night in the rain without even knowing where the girl was to stay, because she had left no address behind, or, if she had left one, it was with the Italian, and the Italian was not giving out any addresses of that kind.

My boy told me how he had roamed the city, checking all the best hotels, thinking one of those would be where the girl would stay, but spotting her finally hours later not in any hotel but walking down the street, making her way absently through the crowd. He said the rain had stopped and the sun was shining, glistening on wet pavement and summer leaves. The top to his car was down. As he saw the girl in the throng of tourists, he jammed on the brakes, stood up, dropping the wheel and shouting out her name wildly. The girl turned and stared. What the girl was doing, my boy told me, was looking for tickets to hear *Così fan tutte*.

The next I heard, they were married. I do not know how my boy managed this. Perhaps, quite simply, he got her with child, or he might have said something that pleased her momentarily. Perhaps he had said that he liked French literature more than Russian, or Russian more than French. Perhaps he took her driving in the dim forest that surrounds that city, and in the gloaming, with the scent of pine in the air, stopped his car suddenly and turned to her, hitting her in the eye with one of those bony elbows, and the girl, momentarily blinded, thought, well, why not? why not this long, loose-limbed American rather than the Italian with the ancient culture, after all? Perhaps she thought, what difference would it make anyway in the end? Perhaps she thought that marriage, like death, was inevitable. Perhaps she thought the rich could afford to be careless.

One thing I know is that she was not in love with my boy. It was quite obvious to me as they walked through the door that summer for a visit, my boy pushing his prize before him proudly, that baby grin spreading wide as all the world. One look at the girl in a narrow, dark blue dress, idly eyeing the magnolia tree and twisting her triple string of pearls around her delicate fingers, and I could see that.

She had the static anonymous prettiness of a porcelain doll. The head appeared too heavy for the slender neck, the big eyes blinked blankly, aquamarine, the teeth glimmered, blue-white. Her allure for my boy lay precisely in the fact that she lacked something, it was obvious to me. It seemed to me that some sort of gauzy veil hung between her and the rest of humanity. What I thought the veil was, at first, was simply stupidity. I was wrong about that. Later I imagined she had suffered some loss in her early years. At times it even occurred to me that she had inherited some fatal strain of fragility that would impair my boy's life.

Day after day, as the summer waned, they lingered on in the rooms at the top of the house. Increasingly uneasy, I began to see that they had little intention of moving on, though my boy was due back at school. Indeed, my boy seemed less and less capable of moving anywhere. When I asked about the future or about his degree, he shrugged his shoulders and told me he was taking a love sabbatical, that he was in no hurry, that they needed nothing, that there was nothing to worry about.

The girl, if she had ever been with child, was no longer so. If any new life had sprung up within her narrow form, it had flickered out fast. I saw no signs of swelling there. Like the head, the body seemed doll-like to me, locked within its white skin, narrow hips, slight childlike curve of stomach, straight stiff legs.

I do not mean to imply that the girl was silent, for that she was certainly not. It was rather as though she had no idea of what to keep to herself and what not. At times she babbled on quite recklessly about her childhood in that savage place, describing with much detail the old rambling house with the courtyards, the verandas, the mangoes and the avocado trees; and about her family, numerous unmarried uncles and aunts, cousins, hangers-on, servants, and even the household pets—there was a monkey, I believe, and a brightly colored parrot that shrieked, Watch out! Watch out! Watch out for thieves!

At other moments she drifted barefoot past me across the tiled floors as though I did not exist at all. She wandered through the rooms indolently, letting her clothes lie where they fell, shutting herself up in the bath for hours, reading Proust. Afterward I found the volume face down on the tiles, the pages wet.

Sometimes at twilight she would appear at the front door, her cheeks flushed with the effort of the climb up the stairs, her arms full of flowers from the market in the town. She would lay out newspaper on the kitchen table and stand before the big glass bowl, carefully arranging the blooms.

Arranging flowers seemed all she knew how to do. Once I asked her to help me prepare an evening meal. I stared at her as she stood obligingly at the sink, turning on the taps fast and watching as the water cascaded onto the lettuce, bruising the leaves. After dinner she sat out on the terrace, gazing up at the stars. It seemed to me that the mosquitoes that devoured everyone else left her alone.

I found myself watching her increasingly on the beach. She

went down to the sea in the heat of the day and lay for a while, half-naked, curled up in the shade. I watched her as she rose and climbed the dunes, picking the white wild flowers that grew in the long grass. Later she filled glass vases with the flowers, which faded fast.

Like some sea creature, awkward on land, she seemed to come alive in the water. She dived from rocks, her body trembling, her skin glistening, her back curving as she entered the water like a lacquered bud. I strained my eyes to see her as she struck out for the horizon, beating straight arms and legs fearlessly, and then letting a wave catch her up, roll her and twist her, and throw her onto the sand, where she lay like some castaway from a strange land.

At night, I was awakened by the sound of someone moving about restlessly, drifting through the rooms. In dreams I saw the girl, a ghostlike figure standing at the iron gate of the garden, her hands on the bars. One night I awoke to hear the sound of her voice calling out my boy's name with what I thought was fear. I heard her sob and say, "It's so dark in here."

As the days passed and the mists rose, covering the beach, the sea, and the sky, I heard my boy's voice rise gradually. Through the thin walls I heard him pacing up and down with long impatient steps. One morning I heard him shout, "Oh, shit! What's the matter with you, anyway?" Once I think he said, "Why can't you, for Christ's sake? Why can't you?" I heard objects fall and shatter on the floor. Once I thought I heard the sound of a blow, a hand against a head.

In the evenings, when the crowds had left the beach, my boy and I sometimes walked together across the sand. We stopped

to admire the sun, setting across the water, the sea and the sky
lit up with color. My boy would disclose very little, however
much I pressed. He walked beside me silently, his long arms
swinging and his head beating back and forth, back and forth,
in time with his steps. Sometimes I would tire, sit for a while,
and my boy would take off running down the beach, wheeling
and coming back to me.

One misty evening as we walked together, he said, "I'm going
back to school this fall."

I said, "You do love her, don't you, darling?" but he turned
and ran off into the mist.

I looked at the gray of the sea and sky, at the bare branches
of trees like the veins of a hand.

I saw them off at the station. They were standing there, stamping
cold feet in the mist. As the train drew in, I turned to the girl
and held her close to me. She was in a white coat with a fur hat
drawn down over her pale eyes. I brushed my lips against her
cheek. Her skin was smooth and cold, her perfume thin and
sweet. She drew back. For a moment I clung to her. She gazed
deep into my eyes. I suppose it was then that I knew what she
lacked and what had drawn my boy to her. I watched as she
turned away and climbed the steps of the train slowly with what
seemed a certain solemnity.

I walked slowly up all those stairs to empty rooms where I
waited with both fear and relief for the news. When my boy
called, he said what I was expecting him to say. He said he
wanted to come home, alone. I said, "Of course, of course, you
can always go back to school in the spring," and put down the
telephone.

I walked out onto the terrace and looked down into the closed garden below, staring into the well of shiny tropical plants and lush green shade. The light in the leaves seemed very bright to me, the blue of the empty sky, perfect. Then I sat down and ate my breakfast. One must keep up one's strength, you know.

IN AMBER

Here she lies, looking as though she were asleep—does she not?—lying under the gauze of the mosquito net, in the strange light of this shuttered room. Would you care to sit a while by her side? You are the first to arrive and, as such, sir, will be my special guest. This iron bed where she lies, with the bars at the head and at the feet, is a bed that belonged to my great-grandmother, you know; it is also the bed where I was born. Now my wife lies here, unmoving, a picture of innocence and peace—not so? Notice how the faint lamplight glimmers on her white neck, lights up her wavy hair, catches the lilt of a thigh. A beautiful woman—is she not?—as beautiful as a Botticelli.

Perhaps you are right: more beautiful than a Botticelli.

Let me draw the curtains over the windows to keep the room cool and dark. I have always liked the rooms of this house kept dark, with the shutters tightly closed against the sun and the air and the view of these flat fields. I carry this land in my head; I have no need to look. I know each branch, each footpath, each blade of grass. This place has been ours, of course, for as long as the white man has been here.

I was always telling her that closed shutters keep a room cool, that dust and sunlight suck the colors from fabrics, warp the furniture, and that open windows are just an invitation for flies, and flies, of course, bring disease. One has to be particularly careful with flies in a place like this, does one not? One never knows where the flies might have been: the suppurating eyes, the open wounds, the compost heap. But she insisted on fresh air, on sunlight. She would walk around this room half-naked, with the curtains open, visible to any native or passerby. As for the flies, she maintained flies never came near her. She said she had no need for this mosquito net. Insects, she insisted, feared her. She often boasted that she was never ill, never caught cold or ran a fever. It is true that she had a remarkable appetite, did she not? I would watch her eat, fascinated. She liked eggs, fish, meat—huge quantities of meat, it seemed to me, eating it half-raw, picking the bones. Once, I found her lying like this in this bed, propped up on those big, white, lacy pillows, her hair loose about her, picking on a lamb bone. And the fruit she could consume! I can see her biting into a granadilla, taking the top off the fruit with those teeth and then tipping back her head and squeezing the juice and pips into her mouth, the orange liquid trickling down her chin onto those heavy breasts.

It never ceased to amaze me, for someone who seemed—how shall I put it?—so full of life—how heavily she slept. She could sleep, it seems to me, endlessly. When I came off the land at noon, I would still find her in this bed, dreaming. She would rise then and bathe, join me on the veranda, half-dressed, her thick hair rapidly braided and hanging like a damp loose rope down her back. She would drink a beer or two, to whet her appetite, she would say. By the time I left to go back to my work, she would be asleep again, sweating in the heat, her hair clinging to her brow. At night sometimes, unable to sleep, I would watch her breasts rising and falling. Ah, such a young and healthy woman, was she not? Whoever would have thought it would come to this? According to the report, she died of something that drained away her strength gradually, leaving her with nothing but the lithe body you see here, and the beautiful face.

In this heat they will not last long.

· · ·

I have always liked the heat, even on the worst of days, when the sun beats down mercilessly on this corrugated iron roof. Perhaps my ancestors came, originally, from some hot country similar to this, and perhaps hers, despite her dark coloring, came from the north. She would sit here on hot days like this, turning pink in the face, fanning herself with that heart-shaped straw fan you can see on the dresser top—I have left everything exactly the way she liked it—gasping for air. How can anyone live in such a climate, she would say. I'm afraid she found this place very boring, you see. Wildlife was of no interest to her, as you must know, and she had no time, she said, for flowers or for trees. What she liked, she would tell me constantly, were people. She liked talking to almost anyone. She would strike up a conversation with a perfect stranger. In the evenings, when I came back into the house, I often found her lounging at the kitchen table, chatting to the cook. When she wanted to, she could talk very well. When she was in the mood, there was no one more charming, was there now? No one I knew seemed able to resist her. You know, she was doing me a favor in letting me serve her, and it would have been impolite to decline.

I was never impolite, I assure you.

It was she who persuaded our neighbor to sell me that field. Nothing grew. I never understood her wanting those clothes she never wore. She was a generous woman, very generous; the sight of poverty always brought tears to her eyes—she hated, particularly, to see a native suffer. She gave lavish gifts.

Of course, in the end, it was I who paid.

Yes, I am used to the silence here, but it seems to me the silence is slightly changed. It is a different silence now. Things will not be quite the same. Perhaps you find it strange that I can sit here by her side. She always said that she found me tiresome, because I never spoke of what I felt, but now look. She complained that we never went anywhere, but I must manage this estate, you know, and spend my evenings with my books. An ornithologist friend of mine would come to dine with us once a week. I had intended to move on, you know, but where, sir, would I find a house with such thick walls, such tall trees that cast such deep shade? Those eucalyptus, their sickle-shaped leaves shimmering silver in the sun, were planted by my ancestors all around this property, you see; where could I find a place where I could rise at dawn and never be disturbed, never have to hear an unfamiliar sound?

Oh, I knew she was not happy. But who is, after all?

The breasts, do they interest you? If you look at them carefully, you may actually find, as I do, that they are rather too large.

I was so very nice to her, sir. I took every measure, you know.

All this is, therefore, very surprising to me. I see no need for the report, for the investigation. Do you not agree?

Must you leave so soon, sir? Before you go, do give yourself a treat and taste her plum cake.

ADULTERY

Under a chestnut tree she stood by his side, facing me. She was tall, pale, with dark hair and dark luminous eyes, the lids half-lowered, sultrily. She wore a black hat with a wide brim, a man's hat. The hat cast a shadow on her face. For a moment I thought the hat slightly vulgar, out of place, a counterrhythm to the woman's elegant silhouette. Then I realized that it was the hat that gave her—the expression that came to mind was—*du chien*, the hat gave her *du chien*.

Though she was slim and narrow-shouldered, I could feel the strength of her languid pose, and when she moved, striding out, long-limbed, in a black sleeveless dress with a single string of pearls dipping between her breasts, my eyes misted.

In the stillness of the garden I could see the smooth green lawn very clearly, the golden tips of the railings, the wings of a white dove fluttering in the heavy leaves of the chestnut tree. I could hear the children's voices coming as if from afar and the coo of the doves.

The one the woman was with, the man by her side, Serge, my husband, I hardly noticed at all, though I was aware that he came up to the woman, put his hands beneath her arms, and let his fingers drift down her body to her waist.

I rose and walked very slowly along the avenues, across the gardens to the other, wooded side, and wandered about there under the trees, glancing up at the white statues of queens long since dead. When I heard the sound of the policeman's whistle at dusk, I left the gardens and walked up the hill toward the Pantheon. The evening air was cool and stung my bare neck, and I felt tired, but I turned up the collar of my jacket and went on walking, loitering in front of shop windows, staring inside, and not really seeing what was there. I did not think of anything but of how long the days were at this time of year, of how late it became dark. The district, though I knew it well, did not look familiar to me. It seemed dirtier than I remembered it. The café on the corner where they sold thin pancakes gave off a pungent odor of cheese, and when I looked down the streets I was puzzled to feel no longer quite myself.

I wandered into Notre Dame and stood leaning against the cold stone of a pillar, breathing in the odor of incense and dead flowers. A woman emerged from the shadows slowly, going toward the door, a woman in a felt hat and black dress stopping to dip her fingers into the holy water and cross herself. I followed her. I watched her swing her narrow hips freely, head thrown back, going along the bank of the river, slackening her pace, unzipping her sling bag and then stopping to light a cigarette. I stood by her side and cast a stone into the Seine, the reflection of her face a pale glimmer like the moon on the gray water in the evening mist. I do not recollect what I said to her, perhaps something about the color of the sky, but I know that as I spoke the feeling of strangeness I had felt earlier left me. We stood there, not saying much, smoking and watching the couples strolling in the gray light, arm in arm.

The place where we went was done up to resemble an English pub, ill-lit booths with dark paneled wood, green lamps on the tables, and plastic menus with pictures of sundaes. There was music upstairs on a sort of balcony, and a few couples were dancing slowly to an old melody. Most of the tables were empty. I glanced at the faces of the people; they were the usual ones in a place of this sort. I ordered a whiskey and soda. I do not recall the first part of the conversation. I was watching the woman's pale face, the dark eyes under the brim of the hat, the under-sized, almost childish breasts. I thought she looked as though she had always known me, though all she did at first was lean back and watch the smoke rings she blew from her cigarette and hum a little under her breath in accompaniment to the music.

After a couple of drinks she told me she worked for one of the designers; she sewed. She described some of the gowns she had made, using her hands to show me the forms. We talked about clothes. She examined me appreciatively, exhaling a cloud of smoke. She praised my silk-print dress. I said it was not difficult to dress in Paris. She said she made her own clothes, and when she had the time she sewed for her little boy. She was married, she said, and had a small boy, who had gone to visit her mother in the Midi. I imagined the woman with a small child sitting on her knee, and the child smiling up at her.

She said her husband was very jealous. "You know the type— strong-willed, sort of a rhinoceros. He makes nuts and bolts and struts about the factory in overalls," she said. I laughed.

She ordered us another drink and told me a little story about her husband. She gave his name. He had found her lover hiding in his underpants in their bathtub. I laughed loudly. She glanced at me with appreciation. I asked what happened next. She said her husband had given her a black eye.

I said. "Why did he hit you? Why not your lover?" Now it was her turn to laugh. She asked about me, about whether I had a man in my life. I nodded and looked down at my drink.

"What's he like?" she asked. There was a pause while I thought what to tell her. I shrugged and said, "Well you know what a man—even the best—is worth."

"What does he look like?" she wanted to know.

"On the lean side, grayish hair, blue-gray eyes—or are they gray-blue?—anyway not unattractive, a boyish smile, rather youthful-looking for his age," I said.

"Sounds very attractive," she said, leaning toward me, her eyes bright.

"Oh," I said, "I suppose you could say so."

"Does he dress well? Is he elegant like you?" she wanted to know, devouring me with her eyes.

I admitted, "He certainly spends a lot of money on clothes."

She wanted to know what he did. I mumbled something about his having been in different fields.

"Rich?" she asked.

"He's had his ups and downs," I said.

The woman became full of high spirits. She told me amusing stories, waved her hands in the air, ordered food for us: eggs and bacon and toast. I said I wasn't hungry, but she made me eat from her plate, breaking off pieces of bread and pushing them around on the end of her fork to mop up the egg. She ordered some wine. I asked her if she was trying to get me drunk. I was already rather drunk and sleepy, but she became more and more animated. I watched her waving hands, the suppleness of the fingers. We drank more wine.

Eventually, she asked me to dance. I hesitated a moment, but when she rose and beckoned to me, I followed her. I felt a little uncomfortable, but the few people there scarcely paid any attention to us. She held me so tightly it hurt and whispered hoarsely into my hair, laughed, and rubbed herself against me.

After a while, I got used to it and let myself go, leaning against her. As I danced, I felt something strange stir within me. Tomorrow, I thought, I would think about things. For tonight the music, the woman's body against mine, were enough.

When I came out into the street I caught a glimpse of the moon through the branches of a tree. I said, "You know, the city is beautiful even in the dark."

When I returned home, very late, I saw Serge's lean, questioning face before me in the hall. When he came over to me and lay beside me on the bed, I let him put his hands under my arms, let them slip down to my waist.

A QUIET PLACE

It was the kind of place found in old houses, the kind of place children tell stories about and adults avoid, windowless, cold, the trapped air slightly musty from being long enclosed.

The place in this house was the bathroom, the one under the stairs. It was furnished with fixtures. There was no carpet on the floor, no pictures or even mirrors on the wall, no books, no knickknacks, no plants, absolutely nothing breakable, only the thick oak door with its inside lock and the old bathtub standing on what looked like animal claws gripping onto the tile below.

That morning, when the boy had gone to his classes, the girl took the children into the wild garden, which glistened with the rain of the day before. Stretched out in a deck chair, in a light-colored linen dress, legs crossed at the ankle, she read a nineteenth-century novel, turning the pages fast, brushing a tear from her eye from time to time. When the elder child called to the girl, she looked up for a moment, noticing the row of trees that grew along the edge of the river, willows, not the weeping kind, but straight tall trees with silver leaves rustling and shimmering, whole boughs rocking back and forth so that they seemed to her to stir the pale sky. She may have watched the river whipped by the wind glinting in the white light of the early spring day. She caught a glimpse of the children running about, half-disappearing in the long grass of the orchard, flitting through the light and shade of the unpruned fruitless trees, their white cotton bonnets drawn down over their ears, their smocked matching sundresses rising like wings of white organdy around their arms. The children bobbed and weaved, fluttering about in the wet grass like butterflies.

The girl went on reading. The elder child called out. The girl read to the end of the page, then said, "I'm coming, I'm coming," sighed, marked her place carefully, and wandered languidly after the children. When she caught up with them the girl pushed them, first one, then the other, on the swing, chanting to them, though only the elder child could hear the words. What the girl chanted was a rhyme she half-recalled: *"How do you like to go up in the air, up in the air so blue, I do think it is the pleasantest thing ever a child can do."* She pushed as hard as she could, sending the children flying up into the air, their thin skirts blown back over their upturned faces, bare toes reaching for the sky. Then the girl went back to her chair and her book in the shade of the laburnum tree, followed by the elder child, who held onto her mother's skirt. When the girl was settled in her chair and had taken up her book, the elder child, the one who could hear, tugged on the girl's hand. She said to the girl, "Mummy, Mummy! Look!"

The girl said, "What *is* it now!"

"Look, look at her," the elder child said, pointing to her sister, who, left alone in the long silent grass, had bent down to scoop up the damp earth in handfuls and throw it up over her head. She was crouching down, rooting in the mud, eating the earth.

The girl got up out of her chair and hastened to pick the younger child up, pry open her small fingers, brush her off. The girl said, "Keep still, will you, keep still for a moment. Why is it that you can never keep still for even a moment, not even for a single moment." She replaced the plug that had fallen from an ear, smelling the sour smell that was given off by the plug.

The child lifted her hand and smeared the mud across the girl's cheek and into her mouth. The girl smacked the child's hand. The child screamed. The elder child, watching with big eyes, sucked her second finger hard.

The girl, holding the squirming, screaming younger one under an arm, ran a bath in the downstairs bathroom, bending over, twisting on both taps as far as they would go, sprinkling in the bath salts, the mauve powder floating down like fine ashes through the dim air. Only a pale yellow light came from the ceiling.

The girl swung the plump naked child from the floor into the bath. Fine grains of gray mud settled to the bottom of the tub. The child, slumped in the water, became suddenly quiet, lolling, letting her blond head go back against the worn enamel of the tub, making little pats on the surface of the water with her hands and watching as the water splashed up.

It was very quiet there. You could hear the wind through the thick oak door. As the girl knelt by the bath, soaping a scrubbing brush, the child leaned forward to catch at her long rope of pearls, twisted the pearls between her fingers, pulled them to her, and tried to suck. The girl pried the child's fingers loose and continued to scrub the mud off her as she wriggled.

"Dirty, dirty baby," the girl said.

When the girl let go, the child reached for the taps and turned the water on again. She put her face under the faucets, so that the water splashed on the floor and on the girl's dress.

The elder child sat on her hands on the lavatory seat and stared at her sister in the bath.

As the girl lifted the younger child from the water she noticed the child's skin was pink from the heat of the water. She bound the child around tightly in a thin white towel and held her still a moment, feeling her solid body.

After lunch the girl put the elder child down for a nap and left the younger one in her high chair in the kitchen. Then the girl took out the plastic cups, the puzzle, and the pictures from the cupboard and sat down facing the child, who banged her fists on the steel tray of the high chair. The girl began piling up the plastic cups, placing one cup on top of the other, carefully, on the tray of the high chair. She said, "Up, up, up."

The child scattered the cups onto the black and white linoleum floor. The girl got down on her hands and knees to pick up the cups, saying at the same time, "Down, down, down, the cups go down." She stayed down there a while, looking for the smallest of the yellow cups on her hands and knees on the dirty linoleum, while the child screamed and kicked her pink toes against the tray of the high chair.

Then the girl took out the puzzle with the animals in their separate slots. She went through the dog that said woof-woof, the cat that said miaow-miaow, the pig that said oink-oink, and the duck that said quack-quack. Then the girl picked up the little white lamb, held it up in the air, and asked the child, "What does the lamb say?"

The child screamed and grabbed the lamb and put it into her mouth and closed her teeth. The girl put her fingers between the child's teeth and extracted the wet lamb.

The girl said, opening her mouth wide and shaking her head, "The lamb says baaaah." The girl opened her mouth wider and bleated at the screaming child, "The lamb says baaaah." Then she pulled the child from the high chair, the child's feet catching on the steel tray and the puzzle falling to the floor. The girl carried the child to her room and put her down on her bed for her nap.

The girl lay down on the sofa in the living room with her book. She tried to read for a while but what she kept thinking was how she had told her school friends that she wanted six children. She had told all her school friends she would have six children, keep them all at home, and teach them herself. She would never send them to school. They would all run around and play games all day long. Soon the book fell from her fingers to the floor, and she rose and went to the bedroom.

Dusk was falling, and the sky was a violet-blue as the girl lay on the four-poster bed and fell asleep. She dreamed of the younger child drowning. The child was sinking down slowly through the clear water of the sea. She could see the child sinking, arms lifted, head thrown back, bubbles rising to the surface of the water. The girl saw herself diving down into the water to catch the child. She dived down again and again, swimming along the bed of the sea, looking for the child, her lungs bursting. Again and again she was forced upward, scissor kicking, seeking air. She was unable to hold her breath for long enough to find the child on the bed of the sea.

When she woke, gasping for breath, she rose and went to the younger child's room. The child was not on the bed or anywhere in the room. The girl heard something moving about downstairs in the living room. She pulled on a gown and descended the stairs.

In the living room the child had torn out the pages of the girl's leather-bound book and spread them around her in a circle. She was stamping methodically on the pages with her bare feet.

The girl caught the child by her arm, wrenching her up so that she hung in the air, bits of paper stuck between her toes. Then the girl let the child drop to the wooden floor with a thud. The girl raised one hand to strike the crumpled child, saw herself, a pale, young woman in a creased blue dressing gown, standing in the middle of a living room about to hit a child who stared up at her, trying to cling to her legs.

It was at that moment that the thought came to her. She thought of a quiet place for the child.

She sat down and tried to piece the book together. She tried to smooth out the crumpled pages and put them back in order. She could hear the child's high-pitched screams and the beating on the door. Finally she stood up. She walked slowly down the corridor to the bathroom under the stairs.

She turned the handle of the door, but the door did not open.

She turned the handle of the door right and left, right and left, right and left. She beat with both fists on the door. Inside, the child wailed and beat on the door. The girl screamed as loudly as she could at the thick door and mouthed the words carefully, as though, if she screamed loudly enough, if she enunciated clearly enough, the child might just hear her words. She told the child to turn the lock, to please try to understand that the child had locked herself in, that it was not the girl who had locked the child in from the outside, but instead the child who had accidentally locked herself in from the inside, that she had only to turn the inside lock the other way, had only to turn the inside lock to the left rather than to the right in order to be free, in order to step right out of the bathroom into her mother's arms.

The elder child came down the stairs in only her underpants. She cried out, "Let her out, Mummy!"

The girl dragged her short nails across the paint of the door. She beat on the door with her knuckles. She threw her slight weight against the heavy door. She ran up the stairs to the bedroom. She snatched up her handbag from the arm-chair. She scratched in the depths of her cream leather handbag. She turned the contents of the handbag onto the floor. She stood staring at them as though she had never seen them before.

She could hear the screaming and the beating on the door.

She went down the stairs to the kitchen and flung open the back door. She picked her way barefoot across the gravel, going to the toolshed beside the garage and pulling down the dusty toolbox from the shelf, spilling the contents on the gravel as she went back to the house. She went back down the corridor to the bathroom and tried to squeeze the tips of her fingers under the door.

The younger child's voice had become faint.

The elder child tried to cling to the girl, but the girl gave her a push that sent her flying.

When the boy entered the house, he found the girl and the elder child huddled in the corridor against the shut door.

He started to say something. The girl dragged herself to her feet, mouthing words. The elder child explained the situation succinctly. The girl called out the name the boy and the girl used for one another. "Oh Noooo," she said and reached out to cling to the boy.

The boy said, "Poor Noo," and took her into his arms and stroked her hair.

MIRROR, MIRROR

The odd thought struck me—obviously a passing fancy—that I had before me, leaning over me, breathing down on me, Snow White's stepmother. I was looking for the long red nails when it became apparent to me that the woman was speaking, actually saying, "What you need now is a little distraction." This was said with what appeared to be a certain urgency. And it was of course not Snow White's stepmother who was voicing this opinion, but Fiamma de Guernay.

I blinked up at the woman.

"It will keep your mind off it," she said.

I said, "What sort of distraction do you suggest?"

"The Granoffs are looking for someone. I think you would be most suitable." The woman rapped her silver-topped cane against the bars of the hospital bed.

Fiamma de Guernay was tall, thin, uncompromisingly hook-nosed. She was studying me out of dark, red-lashed eyes. Her black silk blouse was cut low over a milk-white, freckled bosom of youthful aspect, but the face was old, especially the eyes, I thought, ancient, and the hair, catching the light, had a reddish glow, drawn back from the face in a knot.

It was that time of day when, in that place—which was the place where one would go in those days, in such situations, if one had the means to—the sky suddenly clears after hours of mist, and the sun shines forgivingly on the wet earth. Outside the room, rooks cawed, and other people's babies cried. There were roses growing up a wall, pink roses. There was a pine tree standing in the driveway.

"I think you'd be exactly what the Granoffs are looking for," the woman said again and asked me if I knew this couple she called the Granoffs.

I shook my head, trying to keep my mind on the pain. I had the impression I could make it disappear if I could concentrate enough.

She said she was certain that I must know this couple, must, at least, have heard of Serge Granoff. S.G., she said, was really a very important fellow in his way. She said simply everyone knew the two of them. She was quite amazed that I did not know them and was quite certain that when I had come to my senses I would most probably discover that I did know them. In her opinion I must have met the Granoffs somewhere, sometime, but that if I had not met them, then I must meet them as soon as possible, as she was quite certain they would absolutely adore me. According to Fiamma, the Granoffs were a most charming couple, or a most fascinating couple, or a most elegant couple— she may even have gone so far as to say a most seductive couple. She told me that they kept themselves on the go, that they wintered in Provence or in southern Italy, and that they kept a place up in Paris. She said that the Granoffs were always rescuing some young genius or other, taking him in or giving him a leg up, that they were most generous people and would give you the shirts off their backs, and that in her opinion the recipients were not often as grateful as they ought to have been. In fact, she added, she had noticed that people were often not in the least grateful. On the contrary, it was a case of biting the hand that feeds one, she remarked, while drawing up the thick eyebrows, shaking her head, and looking down at me.

I shifted around uncomfortably in the bed.

Sitting in bright sunlight, Fiamma de Guernay said all of this and probably much more to me. She remarked that like everyone else, the Granoffs had had their share of tragedy. She began gathering up her voluminous handbag, her shawl, her air cushion, and her cane in preparation for a move. As she went toward the door, she hesitated for a moment, turned her head to me, and concluded that I really must meet the Granoffs just the instant I got out of here.

I waited for her in the garden in the shadow of a tree, my shoes in wet grass. Yellow leaves transparent in the light fell around me. Bars, to keep intruders out or to keep patients within, shadowed the windows. The red brick building, they had told me, was very old, though no one seemed to know exactly when it had been built or for what purpose. It perched somewhere on the side of the hill between the lake and the sky and hovered above me in the gray-blue morning air. A long row of thin cedar trees lined the driveway and looked, I thought, like a line of mournful patients waiting to be discharged.

I listened for the sound of her car, but all I could hear was the cawing of the rooks. Suddenly she appeared as if out of nowhere. She came across the lawn. Her head beat back and forth like a metronome, I thought, keeping time to her stiff steps. The cane rapped dully on the ground. Her stockings brushed against one another ominously. She came across the smooth grass in narrow handmade shoes. At that instant, as the light caught the red in her hair, it occurred to me that all of this, like the shiny apple, promised nothing favorable. Somehow this thought and perhaps the effect of the pills added to the strangeness of her sudden presence in that quiet place. I said her name, Fiamma, as though trying it out on her. She kissed me quickly, her cheeks waxy, her perfume narcotically sweet. She settled herself beside me on the air cushion, wrapped the scarf around her shoulders, arranged the folds of her pleated skirt, and twisted the triple string of pearls around her neck.

I stared at the neatly terraced hills, the gray-blue sky, and the smooth white water of the lake, which spread before me in the glare of the early-morning light. Everything seemed to me coated with a lacquer of brilliance, each branch, each blade, each leaf. I took out my sunglasses from the pocket of my jacket. The pain was muted by the pills. I said, "It's very good of you to come."

She said in her deep, singsong voice—she had never quite lost her southern accent—"I spoke to the Granoffs about you last night. According to them, they're known to you and Peter. Are you still quite sure their name doesn't ring a bell?"

"Perhaps I was mistaken," I said.

She told me that they had just got back to their place from wherever it was they had summered. I must, she declared, see the Granoffs' place. She was certain that I could not imagine anything much grander than the Granoffs' place. She would give an arm and a leg, she maintained, to have a place like that rather than the place she had, the place she called, drumming out the *d*'s, a dreadful, dilapidated, drafty château that was perpetually in need of repair. She never had enough money to repair it despite her jewelry, her beautiful jewelry, that she had had to sell for a song. The roof always leaked, the walls always peeled around the baseboards. She said that some people were just not as fortunate as others.

"Just the flowers at the Granoffs' place, ah yes, the flowers! They have irises, they have roses, they have pink, white, and violet sweet peas," she murmured and turned her head from side to side, closed her eyes, and seemed to snuff in the scent of the

Granoffs' flowers. And the trees—the wonderful oak trees—in her opinion no one had trees like that. She told me that at the last reception the Granoffs had given, one of the servants had entwined flowers through the branches of a weeping willow, so that it seemed to have burst forth into flower. She supposed it was one of S.G.'s ideas.

S.G., she said, had the most brilliant ideas; he was an immensely talented man; he was the sort of man who could alter your life or for that matter accomplish just about anything he wished to accomplish. He could paint, he could play the piano, he could write poetry. Naturally, he did not feel it was necessary to fill any run-of-the-mill sort of position, she stated. It would have been rather absurd, would it not, for a man to set out and engage in the ordinary business of earning a living when he possessed such a wife, a wife who had the means that this wife had? Moreover, she went on without stopping, with a half-smile, and with a quick glance at me, lifting thick eyebrows suggestively, putting one hand on my knee, he was a man with a gleam in his eye. Did I know what she meant?

I nodded and said I could very well imagine.

She pulled her skirt a little way up over her knees, exposed long slim surprisingly youthful legs in sheer stockings, an edge of pink petticoat, and a border of lace, and said that, of course, a man of that sort could hardly be expected to be governed by convention.

"What about the wife?" I asked.

She declared, her voice low, deep-throated, "Oh, Lisa. Lisa is a very sophisticated, a very sensible sort of a woman." She said there was no drama with Lisa Granoff, that Lisa minded her *p*'s and *q*'s, she did, that Lisa turned a blind eye when a blind eye should be turned, if I knew what she meant.

I assured her I did.

She said that whatever happened, Lisa Granoff was always imperturbable, was always impeccably turned out, was not pretty, really, no, as much as she liked her, she, Fiamma, could not really maintain that Lisa Granoff was pretty. Fiamma glanced at me and added that prettiness, anyway, to her mind, had never really got anyone anywhere. What a woman needed were wits, and Fiamma de Guernay was quite sure that Lisa Granoff had those. According to Fiamma, one could safely assert that Lisa Granoff was a very distinguished sort of a woman. I must know what she meant. Yes, when everything was said and done, she had a lot of admiration for a woman like Lisa Granoff.

"Besides," Fiamma added, after a pause, lowering her voice and putting up one hand to the side of her mouth, "I don't really think that well-bred women are awfully interested in that sort of thing, do you? Probably—of course I'm only guessing, cannot be in any way certain, never having, naturally, discussed such a thing with Lisa—there were moments when Lisa Granoff was really glad to have S.G. off her hands, so to speak. There can be times when such arrangements suit both parties, don't you think? I don't care what people say, I still maintain that women don't need it as much as men do."

I could feel the dark wool of my dress lapping up the heat. I could see the haze lifting from the valley. The lake and the mountains seemed to merge in the bright light. I could just make out the white seams of snow running down the sides of the mountains. The sun was higher now though still invisible in the white glare. I sat there, looking at the rows of neat Swiss vines going on upward, relentlessly. The pain was distant like a name or a dream one cannot quite grasp. My head felt light, my belt was cutting into my waist, and I had the impression the air around me had grown thin.

When I awoke that evening, she was still there. Without opening my eyes I could smell her heavy perfume. I could hear her moving around, fussing, rearranging the mats on the dressing table, shaking out a fold from a curtain, adjusting the bedspread, or—the thought occurred to me—standing mumbling something before the mirror on the wall.

I said nothing, watching her moving about, and it seemed to me that in that light her skin had a slightly greenish tinge.

She said, "What you want to do is think of it as though it were the measles or the chicken pox. And remember, never expect anything, nothing at all. If you never expect anything, then you can't be disappointed, now can you? I have a wonderful book for you, a complete encyclopedia for the mistress of the house. I must bring it to you. It is absolutely fascinating. There are all sorts of little things one can pick up, you know—things that can make all the difference."

She switched on the light by my bed and shut the curtains with a sharp tug on the cord. She sat down, picked up her voluminous handbag, and opened up her knees slightly to accommodate the weight, her skirt sagging between her legs.

The handbag resembled, I thought, a doctor's bag, with a steel bar along the top and a little padlock hanging down one side. I wondered what she could possibly have found to keep in it. I watched as she leaned over, the lamplight on her hair, drew apart the wide mouth of the bag, and plunged her hand inside, her long nails clicking against hard objects. What she brought forth was a heart-shaped velvet box. She opened the box and

drew forth from a bed of cotton a brooch with small rubies set in
the shape of an *S*. With one quick movement she pinned the
brooch onto my robe. "It's lovely, isn't it? I always wanted you
to have it," she said. She told me that the brooch had been in
her family for generations and that it was one of the few things
she had kept. In her opinion, it was particularly appropriate for
an occasion of this sort.

When I protested that it was too much, that really I could not
accept it, she told me that she had never known which of her
ancestors had a name beginning with *S*, that in fact most of her
female ancestors had been called Fiamma, as she was herself,
as far as she knew, but that surely such an almost magical
coincidence must mean the brooch was destined all along for no
one else but me.

I retreated to the bathroom and locked the door behind me. My
legs trembled; the pain was there again. I sat on the stool
without switching on the light. The moon lit the room. I stared
at the bars on the pebble-glass window, the empty tub standing
on clawed feet, the steel warming pipes for the thin towel, and
the smooth surface of the full-length mirror on the door. I stared
at my own shadowy reflection in the mirror for a while. In the
moonlight, the eyes seemed very dark, and the hair so black it
looked almost the color of ebony. The brooch seemed to glow
with its own light. The wind muttered and rattled the windowpane.

When I came out of the bathroom Fiamma was sitting very
still in the armchair in the corner of the room as though, I
thought, she were hugging the shadows. She declared, if anyone
was to understand my predicament, it would surely be Lisa

Granoff. Fiamma admitted, strictly *entre nous,* that S.G. had rather overstepped the line as far as Lisa Granoff was concerned, that certainly she, Fiamma, would understand that a man like S.G. required more freedom than one would usually grant, and certainly Lisa Granoff had granted S.G. more freedom than one would usually grant, but Lisa Granoff had had to put up with more than most. Fiamma assured me that she did not like to gossip, did not like to speak ill of her neighbor, but that she was obliged to say in all honesty that there had been a few shaky moments in that marriage. She would even go as far as to say that there had been a few shaky moments in her own marriage. Still, she said, looking down at me, drawing herself up, tapping with the cane, fussing with the shawl, and going on in her deep voice, marriage, a family, children, were sacred. She had come to the conclusion that, bad as it might be, and she knew it could be bad, she had herself suffered in the same way—and she had not had my advantages: had not had money or looks or that wonderful appetite, and, as she always told her friends, not a nerve in her body—still, there was nothing to take the place of marriage. When children, a family, were involved, there was no sacrifice that was too great.

When the nurse came into the room, she opened the window and said what I needed was more air. I listened for the sound of the wind in the pine tree, but it seemed to me all I could hear now was the rush and tumble of my heart.

The nurse said I looked very pale and tired, that I seemed to have taken a turn for the worse.

"It's my heart," I said. The nurse held my wrist, counting the beats. She murmured, glancing at Fiamma, that I had probably

not rested sufficiently that day. The nurse said that at times like
these, the people closest to us are not always the most helpful.
The nurse gave me something to drink and plumped up the
pillows.

Fiamma declared that she, Fiamma, could tell just from the
way the nurse touched those pillows what a very excellent nurse
she was, and that Fiamma considered nursing to be absolutely
crucial, that it was nursing that made the difference between life
and death. Fiamma declared she absolutely agreed with the
nurse as far as the subject of visitors was concerned. As for her,
Fiamma, she had been very careful to keep the conversation as
anodyne as possible. Why, she was quite sure she had been
boring her poor daughter-in-law to death with a lot of silly
nonsense about people her daughter-in-law did not even know.
Of course, she, Fiamma, had had a lot of experience with these
sorts of situations, not, naturally, as much experience as the
nurse had had, the nurse being not only an excellent nurse but
a very pretty one and, Fiamma asked the nurse, where on earth
had the nurse found that perfectly darling little pearl ring on her
ring finger?

I listened for the sound of the wind in the tree, but all I could
hear were distant footsteps in the corridor and the faraway sound
of Fiamma's voice. I thought I heard the clanging of a bell, but
perhaps the bell was in my head. I was slipping down some
smooth green slope, weightlessly, as if on wings. I was falling
away. Fiamma's voice came to me now from a great distance,
Fiamma's voice and even the yellow curtains and the flowers by
the bed. For a moment it seemed to me that Fiamma was standing before the mirror and saying my name, but perhaps what she
was talking about was Lisa Granoff. Perhaps what Fiamma was
saying was that Lisa Granoff, even Lisa Granoff, had not been

able to stand up under the strain, and that Lisa Granoff had actually spent some time in the place where I was spending time now. Perhaps Fiamma was saying that she, Fiamma, was one of the few people to know that Lisa had actually considered leaving S.G., but of course such an idea was completely preposterous, was obviously doomed to failure. Because after all, Fiamma may have asked me, where on earth would Lisa Granoff have found a man like S.G.? After all, Fiamma probably asked me, where could Lisa Granoff have found such a handsome, such a distinguished man, a man who could simply walk into a room and command such respect? No, Fiamma could not possibly think of another man who was in any way a match for S.G., except of course for her own darling boy.

Perhaps Fiamma asked me to consider this question as I slipped away softly, no longer trying to hold myself back, doing what I felt was required of me, which was simply to keep sliding, serenely, weightlessly, through the light. What would Lisa Granoff have done during all those long lonely nights? In Fiamma's opinion Lisa Granoff was not the sort of woman to cope with those long lonely nights or all the rest of the things that might seem like nothing at all, but could be found dreadfully difficult, and that a man like S.G. simply took in his stride. Besides, Fiamma went on, as beautifully turned out as Lisa Granoff was, as elegant as Lisa Granoff was, she was no longer young, there was no doubt about that. And it was important, Fiamma probably told me, to face up to the fact that a woman of a certain age was just not in the same position as a man of a certain age. A man of a certain age could go out and, before you knew it, would have found himself a woman ten years, my God, what was she saying, not ten but twenty years younger. After all, and I should make no mistake about it, a man's face at that age, a man's skin

at that age, a man's body at that age were just not in the same
sort of condition as a woman's. Nature, in Fiamma's opinion,
was not kind to women.

In the end, of course, Lisa had come to her senses, Fiamma
probably said, as I slipped away along the bright green slope, a
long slow fall through the light, plunging down with a continuous
forward motion, Lisa Granoff had done what any sensible woman
would do in such a case. She had simply gone out and found
herself a little distraction to keep her mind off it.

ABSENCE

The woman says, "Could you move a little closer?"

I say, "Of course," and shift down toward the end of the table.

There is no window or door in here. The room opens onto a corridor and beyond that onto a vestibule, and beyond that onto a flight of steps. Though I cannot see the steps from here I know they are carpeted in red. Apart from the single naked light bulb in the ceiling directly above me, the room is dark. The faint yellow light encloses my body like a shroud.

A curtain has been swung back along the bar between the two narrow plastic beds. There are no chairs, no table, only a clock on the wall with black hands that seem to have stopped. All I can hear are the light sounds of women's voices murmuring.

The woman rubs her hands together. I feel her lift my wrist. She places one arm by my side, lifts the other wrist and raises the thin white sheet from under me on either side to cover my breasts and legs.

I sleep, or I almost sleep. I hear her saying, "Ah, now I see I do know you."

I cover my eyes with my arm. I say, "Could we turn off the light?"

"We're not allowed to," she says, standing under the light.

Her face is not familiar to me. She looks young, with dark hair drawn back and tied at the nape of her neck. She has thick chapped lips. The buttons at the bottom of her white uniform have been left undone, and I can see her thighs and her dark stockings. She wears elevated shoes with cork soles.

She says, "Well, perhaps I should say I recognize the rings."

. . .

The rings were how they knew who Clea was and who she had been. There was a pearl ring, quite unscratched and still firmly fixed in its diamond setting, and there was a yellow diamond one, still brilliant, still glimmering. They put the rings in a plastic bag with what was left of her handbag, her dress, and her high-heeled shoes. They spoke in whispers, politely, careful to make sure we had everything that remained.

I said to the man I would like to see her, but he said to me, "If I were you I wouldn't look."

The woman asks, "Is there anything I should look out for?" Her skin is so white she looks as though she has always been in this room.

I shake my head. "No."

She says, "No sore spots?"

"No sore spots," I say.

She begins with the left hand. She takes the arm out from under the sheet, takes each finger, starting with the thumb, pulls fast from the joints, snapping her fingers together as she lets go of mine. When she gets to the ring finger she says, "He must love you a lot."

Upstairs in the nursery we lay side by side on twin beds in our vests and pants, the white light of the afternoon sun filtering through chintz curtains, the mosquito nets thrown back over the bars at the ends of the beds. Clea stared up at the ceiling and said, "She's laying out her constitution," and I said, "What's a constitution?" and Clea, "It's a heart and lungs and a stomach."

I asked how a constitution could be laid out, and Clea said Mother's constitution was made of jewels: emeralds, sapphires, yellow diamonds, pearls, and a ruby for the heart, and she spread it out on the grand piano for a rest in the afternoon.

The woman touches my body without looking at me. Without looking at her, I know she touches me and stares at the gray wall as the blind violinists must have stared while others made love.

In October the hedges of May blossomed with flowers that shone like small white diamonds. Up the hill was the junior school, and below was the senior school, and in between lay the hedges and lawns and the trees, wide-spread oak trees and tall eucalyptus. There were beds of stiff cannas that glowed yellow and orange in the sun. Clea walked from the senior school to the junior school to wash out my hair and my toilet things, to brush my hair until the sparks flew, saying she liked my straight coarse hair. I told her I liked her soft curls, but I thought my hair was better than hers.

The woman entwines her fingers with mine like a lover's. She bends my fingers back as far as they will go. Then she works on the arm from the wrist up to the shoulder, moving her hands with a circular motion forcefully but with a slight tremble in the tips of her fingers. She lifts back the sheet to uncover each part of the body, pressing down hard except on certain parts.

. . .

When we walked on the lawn, it was winter, and the grass was yellow and stiff. Clea told me about men until I laughed and said it was not true. "But it is," she said. "Cross my heart," she said. I threw myself down onto the grass laughing, but she said to get up immediately, that it was no laughing matter.

The woman says, "You can turn around now," and turns me over onto my stomach with a little push and plants me facedown. She begins working on the back.

On the train, Mother's hat trembled, and she waved her ringed hands, the diamonds catching the light as she said, "Why are you girls telling me this now, what am I supposed to do about this now, stop the train? You girls have no idea how difficult it is to bring up two girls without a man." As we went through a long dark tunnel, the train rocking and shrieking and everyone shouting loudly, a suitcase falling from a rack, I smacked someone's cheek in the dark.

The woman says her husband is a police officer. She says he once accidentally cracked a rib while saving a man's life, and afterward the man sued him. She says that because of the nature of his work he's distracted sometimes.

The butcher, the baker—someone once told me butchers, because of the cutting nature of their work, were accorded clemency if they committed a crime; not that Clea's man was a butcher; he was of

*the educated kind: blue-eyed, blond, with a slim body that looked
hard like the face, and very good with hearts, so to speak. They
are often good with hearts out there. They take a heart from the
almost stiff and put it in the almost quick. Clea's heart man said
the difficulty was not so much exchanging the hearts but finding
the right ones to exchange.*

The woman beats my buttocks with hands as stiff as boards. I
think she could probably kill someone with those hands. She
could snap your wrists and ankles.

*Mother said that I wouldn't believe what had happened, that
Clea's man had gone and turned her flower garden into a cabbage
patch, and when I asked if she was not imagining things, she said
that no one would imagine cabbages, not a sea of cabbages, not
cabbages stretching as far as the eye could see.*

The woman takes my head in her hands and rubs her fingers in
my hair. They make the sound of waves on the sand. She rubs
my scalp gently, around and around.

I wonder if the woman let her hands wander freely into the
darkness what I would say. What if she were to lay her head
down across the deep chasm that encloses the heat within me?
What would happen then?

*Mother said it was the sauna she was worrying about now, the
sauna door that could be locked from the outside. She said she*

wondered what he would do next, what Clea could do to protect herself.

The woman has been talking to me while I was sleeping. Perhaps she has been talking because of the silence. Now she says that the policeman has a child from a first marriage, a frail blond boy. She says the boy waits on the steps for his mother. She says that she can hardly be expected to be the boy's mother, can she?

Mother said, "Black and blue, black and blue," and I said, "No, oh no," and Mother said, "I'm telling you, black and blue." I remembered picking mulberries in the garden and smearing our faces with the purple stain, and sitting in front with Clea behind me, her legs around my waist and using our hands like paddles, sailing around the bath, visiting foreign countries, going "Overseas," going around and around the big tin bath with the feet like claws, the water splashing on the floor. I remembered picking flowers in the garden to make garlands for our heads and our waists and our ankles and our wrists and dancing on the lawn thus bedecked, and lying at night with our legs in the air waiting for the nanny with the Vaseline jar and lying head to head on the concrete around the pool, taking off our water wings and touching tongues in the sunlight.

The woman tells me to take a nice deep breath, that's it, to breathe. My head rests against her stomach. Our eyes evade one another. Perhaps I do remember the face; I suppose we must have done this before.

. . .

The man lifted his eyebrows and scratched the side of his eye, saying, all right, if I insisted, but it would take a moment. He left me standing in the circular room, clutching the plastic bag with the rings, looking at the sunlight on the floor, which was made of marble or some kind of reddish stone and dipped slightly in the middle as though there were a drainage system there.

The woman leans across me so that her breasts touch me. Leaning across me to adjust the sheet, she brushes her body against me.

They had wrapped her up in a sheet that seemed gray to me, but perhaps it was not the sheet but the skin that was gray. The eyes were closed, the nose and the small chin were tilted slightly toward me so that I thought of the Arab women in purdah, and the word that came to me was obedient, *as though Clea were tilting up her face to me to show me what I had come to see.*

I rise from the plastic bed. I wrap the sheet about me. I turn the rings around. I walk down the corridor and into the vestibule to dress.

THE GARDEN
PATH

When the telephone rang we were sitting on the terrace having a drink. He had his feet up on the straw table next to the silver tray with the cut-glass decanters and the tumblers. I was eating one of those delicious little green olives with the pimento in the center, you know the kind I mean. I wiped my fingertips on the lawn napkin and stubbed out my cigarette. I sighed and said to him, "Just a minute, love," and came inside to pick up the phone.

I stood leaning against the jamb of the terrace door and said, "How *are* you, darling? Lovely to hear your voice." I said, "Just hang on a sec, now," put down the telephone and picked up my whiskey and soda and had a quick swig. I slipped my cigarettes into the pocket of my skirt and raised my eyebrows significantly at him.

"Now tell me how you are, sweet," I said to her, and glanced up at the darkening sky. It was a fine evening, I thought, an evening for sitting on the terrace with a drink.

"I'm all right," she said in a low voice.

"You don't sound all right," I said and had another sip of whiskey, lifted a hand in the air toward him with resignation, and sat down in the chair by the phone. I said, "How're the boys?"

"I keep losing them. I spend my time chasing them from the basement to the attic," she said.

"Good heavens, I certainly hope you find them," I said, watching my boy through the door pour himself another drink.

"Oh, of course I find them. I usually find them sitting in the street looking bored. Why is it that French kids don't play in the street?" she said.

"You don't sound too good to me. You don't sound too good at all. Are you sure you're all right?" I asked.

"I haven't been feeling too good, actually. I find this difficult. That's why I called," she said.

I said, "Darling, I *know* how difficult it is. You're talking to the right person, let me tell you. And please call me anytime, day or night. Just you call me whenever you want to. I know how you feel. I've been there, too."

"I don't like to bother you," she said.

"Of *course* you're not bothering me," I said.

He was striding up and down across the terrace in his gray flannels and his blue blazer, his head bent forward.

She said, "It's just that there doesn't seem to be anyone here I can really talk to."

"Poor darling. You know what you *really* ought to do? Would you mind if I told you what I thought you should do?" I said. "You really ought to get some professional advice. I mean, it's no good upsetting your mother, as I've said before. What you need is a professional."

"Professional advice?"

"Well, of course, you can call me anytime, darling, you know that. But I can't really be objective, can I? I mean I try, but obviously I can't. I mean I'm just too close to you *both*," I said and glanced at him, waving my empty glass in the air.

"You seem *very* objective to me," she said.

"I do my best," I said, while he refilled my glass.

"You mean someone like a doctor, don't you?" she said.

"Well, yes. *Everyone* goes to a psychiatrist at some time or another. Why, I went for years when I was in a similar situation."

"I don't think I'd want to do that," she said.

"Why on earth not?" I said, and waved my unlit cigarette at him through the door.

She said, "I don't know. I'd keep thinking of Mother saying they lead you down the garden path."

"That sounds dreadfully old-fashioned to me. I mean if I had your money I'd probably go myself, though I don't suppose they'd be able to do much with me at my age," I said and laughed.

She said, "Oh, I don't know. After all, what can they really *do?*"

"Of course, it can be difficult. I remember that woman I saw, she spent her time doing tapestry. *Tapestry,* can you imagine! She just sat there and sewed and sewed. She sewed away while I was pouring out my heart. It drove me quite crazy. But you're different. You're so *brave.* You've been so *splendid* about all of this. Really, I admire you," I said rather loudly as he lit my cigarette.

"I don't think I've been very brave."

"Oh, you've been a soldier, really you have. I don't know who else would have put up with what you've put up with. Now you just listen to me. Call the American hospital and get a list of names. Tell them you want the kind that *talks.* Remember that. You don't want someone who just sits there and grunts. Promise me you will, or I'll die of worry," I said.

"You're awfully good to worry so," she said.

"Well, darling, you know why I do it, don't you?" I said and glanced across the terrace.

She said, "My God, you should see the waiting room," and giggled a little bit. I was lying down with a migraine with the shutters drawn and a cold compress on my forehead when she called.

"What about the waiting room?" I said, "You sound better already."

"My God, *cherubs* floating across a blue sky!" she said.

I said, "Cherubs?" and opened my eyes for a moment and then shut them again.

"He's got these little fat cherubs painted on the ceiling in the waiting room."

I said, "What's the man look like?"

She said, "I don't know. I don't think I really looked."

I said, "You must have seen something, for goodness' sake."

She said, "I suppose he has thickish dark hair, dark eyes."

I said, "Sultry-looking, would you say? Did you find him attractive?"

She said, "I don't know. I mean, I was nervous and hardly looked at him."

I said, "Well, what did he say? What did he say you should do? I hope you've got the kind that tells you what to do."

"Oh, he talks all right," she said and giggled a bit again. "He wanted to know about my sex life. I almost fell off my chair. Literally, I felt the room spin around me," she said.

I said, "What else did you talk about? Did you tell him about the problem, at least? Did he give you some advice?"

"He didn't seem very interested in *that*. I told him, of course, and I thought he looked rather bored. He gave a little yawn. I suppose he's heard it all before. I suppose it happens all the time. He wanted to know how long I'd been married, if I'd known any other men. I told him I'd only known one," she said.

I waited for her to go on.

She said, "I don't think I'll go back. After all, what can he do for me?"

I said, "You sound better, at least. He can't be all bad. I'm sure he'll think of something."

The next time she called we were dining on the terrace. She was giggling rather hysterically, I thought. She kept saying, "You won't believe this."

"I won't believe what? I really don't know what you find so very funny. Life doesn't seem all that funny to me, particularly at this moment," I said and looked across the table at him, toying with his glass. I said, "What *are* you talking about?"

"That psychiatrist, of course," she said.

"What happened with the psychiatrist?" I asked.

"That man, that silly little *man*," she said and laughed again. "Do you really want to know? Are you sure you want to hear this?"

I said, "He didn't actually . . ." and pushed my plate to one side.

She said, "Yes he did. He actually did."

I watched him rise and walk over to the table and pour himself another glass of wine.

I said, *"Well,* I really don't know what to say. As I said before, they do all sorts of things these days."

"This was something else," she said.

I said, "Wasn't there one of those early analysts who went in for that sort of thing: Ferenczi, was that the man's name? A brilliant man, wasn't he?"

She said, "I think I recall something dreadful happened to him."

"Listen to me: the main thing is that you are feeling better. You *are* feeling better, aren't you?" I said and saw him drop his knife on the floor.

PERMUTATIONS

1) The Couple in the Garden

Their shadows at her feet, S. sees the man and the woman reclining in deck chairs at some distance from one another, sipping tea from shell-shaped cups under the burning void of a white sky, the lawn stretching out seemingly without end, falling in smooth heavy folds, dark green and all-encompassing, and beyond this the pebbled driveway lined with oaks, the branches almost touching, casting deep violet shadows on the stones, the air filled with the cloying fragrance of honeysuckle, as S. breaks the stillness of the day, and watches as the woman turns languorously and says, "I like the sound of her voice," whereupon the man seems to stare at S. from behind dark glasses and raises thin eyebrows and nods, his impassive face almost kind, S. thinks, while the woman calls upon S. to demonstrate her suitability, so that S. invents something and would have invented more but finds herself gazing at the garden and the man, who is lighting a cigarette with a quick-firing flame, almost invisible in the brilliant light, his nails yellow, and the sun catching the red stone of the gold signet ring on his ring finger, and the man drawing smoke deep into his lungs and letting it out again slowly, the skeins of smoke emanating from the uneven, yellowish teeth while the man removes the sunglasses idly with his finger and thumb, and S. sees his eyes like blue beryl, and the riding crop with the gold claw handle lying on the grass by his side and the leprosy-white skin, and S. thinks she will certainly decline whatever might be offered, although no offer seems likely, the man staring with an expressionless glance that seems to slip over her, like water slipping over a lacquered surface, and still S. stands transfixed, bereft of words, until the woman, who is tall, pale, and red-lipped and appears to belong else-where like the man—looks indeed like a younger version of the man—lifts up one long-fingered hand, murmurs something, S. thinks, about a difficult assignment, staring, S. imagines, at S., though all S. can see is a distorted reflection of her own face in the dark of the woman's glasses, as the woman uncoils herself slowly with a boneless movement and glides across the grass.

2) The Man

Standing and facing the man at the height of the heat, heels digging into soft grass, the glare of the white light in her eyes, the orange sun beating down on her head, S. tries to shift her weight forward onto her toes and sweats, her mouth dry, feeling faint; she would like to sit, but this man only lifts the riding crop from the grass, watches it cut the air, holds it in both hands across his knees and bends the leather so that it arches, and goes on smoking his filter-tipped cigarette, while S., barely able to stand, moves toward the deck chair where the woman sat, the man flicking his crop toward the chair where S. sits down, the sun crossed with clouds like bars, S. thinks, as the man leans, his pale forehead almost touching hers, asking is she dizzy, and not to worry, that they almost always feel that way the first time they come up into this thin air, but that she'll soon get used to it if she stays, whereupon S. says that she will be going if there is nothing else the man wishes to know, the man laying his crop across his knees and saying there is just one thing, would S.

happen to know any lines by heart, staring so that S. feels her
cheeks redden and sees the flash of the stone, her past fading as
the once-heard words rush to her, the sun blazing, a bird flying
darkly against the white sky, running through the words *Water,*
water everywhere, going on breathlessly but without error to
About my neck was hung, and attempts to rise from her chair,
but the sun or the man's gleaming eye holds her, so that she
sinks deeper into her chair, whereupon the man, whose face is
in the shadow and seems to grin, says that a cup of tea might be
of help, but says this without making any move, so that S.
scrapes her chair across the grass and leans over and pours
herself a cup of strong tea and milk, the tea slopping into the
saucer, S. leaning down to sip the tea noisily and watch the man,
who lifts his fine eyebrows and jiggles his shiny moccasins so that
the tassels dance on the high arch of his narrow feet, and as S.
looks at the pale skin of the man's hairless chest, she thinks she
hears a cry coming from the house in the distance, perhaps a name
called out, but when she looks across the lawn, all she sees are
the windows, like fragmented mirrors reflecting the blue of the
sky, and she feels the man's hand cold on her knee.

3) The Woman

The woman asks whether S. likes reading aloud, because the
woman *adores* being read to, prefers the as-if, the land of myth
and heroes, and likes to get beyond herself, lounging on the love
seat, long legs folded with no apparent effort beneath her, leaning back into thick cushions, speaking in a low voice, and
without enunciating clearly, so that S. leans toward her, and
their shoulders almost touch when the woman pours a drink from

the decanter, and although S. calls out no, no, the woman goes
on pouring and talking while S. looks around the screened
porch; what she sees is the chaise longue under the window, the
rosewood Queen Anne desk with the blue writing paper and
letters in the pigeonholes under the drop leaf, and an old rag
doll, propped up against the wall, dressed in the costume of
some other time and place, the head of the doll falling on its
chest, and S. sips the drink, heavy-headed, the woman sitting
immobile, gazing out and murmuring something about the
house, the vast garden, and about the emotions engendered by
such immense spaces, and S. looks at the land rising and falling,
the solitary banana tree at the end of the lawn, its ragged leaves
moving slowly in the slight evening breeze, the sky a still red,
the pool with the long reflections of trees in water, while the
woman's words—or the drink—weigh S. down like a stone, and
the woman says something about summer coming so strangely at
Christmas, about this place that seems without a past and probably without a future, and about its making her feel empty or
barren, and while the woman speaks to no one, or to no one in
the room, S. thinks, the woman's eyes glitter strangely, though
S. is not sure if it is the eyes, or just the effect of the fading light
of the late afternoon, and S. watches as the woman weeps silently, tears on her gaunt cheeks, and S. looks down at the
woman's hand, the fingers closed tightly, the knuckles white,
and covers the woman's hand with her own.

4) The Portrait

As S. rises, the woman takes her by the hand and says that she
must have a look at the room, S. protesting but being held fast,

dragged onward through the maze of muffled rooms, childlike, she thinks, as she tries to linger, admiring long vistas through double doors, her head spinning as she follows the woman through the endless rooms of the house from the blue hush of the bedroom down carpeted stairs through gold and white reception rooms across an inner courtyard where the dark leaves of the avocado fleck the stone, and S. watches the sun dipping and the moon moving into the sky, while going on through clanging kitchens and pantries, rooms opening onto other rooms for no apparent purpose other than to please, rooms filled with glittering French pieces perched uselessly, S. thinks, exotic birds with their wings clipped, gilded clocks decorating marble mantelpieces, sofas and chairs covered in petit point, bowls and old brasses reflected in polished surfaces, the woman dipping and rising before her until they come to a hallway draped with damask, where S. glimpses a portrait of a woman in white, with an ostrich feather in her hair and a gold slave bracelet around her smooth upper arm, and S. manages to linger, thinking the portrait must be of the woman who owns the house as a young girl, and then thinking no, not this woman who owns this house, but another woman S. has seen a long time ago in another place, and then thinking, heart beating loudly, no, not another woman but herself, S., here in this dim hallway, though why she thinks this portrait of a delicate woman with gold hair a portrait of herself, S., with her heavy black hair, her hazel eyes, and her lightly freckled skin, who carries, she knows, too much weight, and dresses brightly, perhaps even garishly, why she thinks this a portrait of herself in fancy dress, she knows not, and as she lingers, the woman grasps her still more firmly and leads her on, pointing out here the shiny surface of a Steinway—at S.'s disposition, of course—or there a sudden

view of the tennis court, where the morning glory climbs up the
wire—and where the coach comes at four, should S. care to
play—so that S. is not sure, once she has passed the portrait, if
she has seen a portrait of herself, or of this woman, or of some
other woman.

5) The Servants

For Sunday evening, S. thinks, there are many servants in the
house: manservants polishing floors in khaki uniforms, or pushing heavy vacuum cleaners across delicate carpets or rubbing at
the glass of the many-paned windows of the house or cleaning
silver to a high shine; maidservants in white aprons dusting or
kneading dough or washing or ironing with flat irons that they
heat on charcoal fires, and one large maidservant in particular
with a spotless white *doek* on her head and a shiny face panting
through the swing door of the kitchen, who knocks S. over with
the tray of silver, the silver flying to the floor, while the woman
watches, and the maidservant cries out, opening wide her
mouth, tongue flapping like a small white fish struggling to
escape, S. thinks, from the depths of her mouth, as the servant
lumbers down onto hands and knees on the carpet, fumbling for
the silver pieces, and the salt flecks the pomegranate pattern,
and S. is almost crushed by the bolsterlike bosom and trunklike
legs, S. sprawling on the floor, sweating, watching as the servant
heaves herself slowly to her feet and stands over her, panting
like some huge giant, arms full of silver, S. thinks, seeing from
the hunched shoulders and the veiled eyes that this servant,
indeed all these servants, would prefer S. to withdraw, to smooth
down her transparent red muslin and retreat, which is, anyway,

what she has had in mind from the start, and she really cannot think why she is still here, as the woman drags her to her feet, taking S.'s hand to raise her up and brushing off salt from S.'s dress, smoothing down S.'s short, tight dress over her thighs, leading her onward, but not before S. sees the maidservant darting what appears to be a warning glance at her, abandoning the silver pieces and the salt on the floor and disappearing through the swing door with what seems alarming alacrity, as though, S. thinks, the maidservant wishes to put as much distance as possible between S. and herself.

6) The Window

S. watches the woman climb the stairs slowly, stop, look back at S., who now lags behind, raise her handkerchief to her forehead, wiping away some imaginary moisture, for her skin seems to S. a miracle of smooth whiteness, the woman drawing up a minute silver-backed mirror on a chain between her breasts, pressing open the lid with her thumb and forefinger, inspecting herself, lifting her chin, wetting her lips with the tip of her tongue, as S. stares through the small panes of the long window in the staircase, each pane of glass different, as though, S. thinks, the craftsmen who built this white mansion were unable to match the glass, and looking out, S. sees the pine trees lean dangerously near the back of the house and the man walk through the shadows of the trees, seeming older than S. had thought, though S. cannot determine his age precisely; he is white-haired, ravaged and stooped, his elegant clothes curiously too tight in places and in others too loose, his shape wavering and almost humped, so that she thinks there is something not quite in order, something even slightly comical about him, though, as the man opens the small gate that leads from the pine grove to the rest of the garden, S. shifts her gaze to another windowpane and decides the man is nothing if not completely serious, without even a hint of humor, that this man she now perceives, who might almost be a different person, is a man of some distinction, perhaps self-satisfied, even sardonic and cruel, but still a man who knows how to command, a titled man after all, though S. knows nothing of the hierarchy of titles, or how they are acquired, a man with piercing eyes and a certain dignity in his bearing that commands respect, obedience, or even submission, though why S. remains in this man's house she is not at all sure, nor does she know where she might go if she were to leave.

7) The Room

In the chamber on the top floor S. sees no paintings, no photographs, no bottles or jars, no ruffles or valances, no clocks, not even a carpet on the floor, only a brass bed with bars at head and foot with an embroidered counterpane and pillows heaped high and a small table and chair under the dormer window that looks over the land, so that it occurs to S., as the woman lights the bedside lamp, that the couple may fear theft or perhaps have already had things stolen, the woman telling S. to try the bed, and when S. hesitates to lie down on the counterpane, giving S. a little push so that S. sinks down into the pillows, and closes her eyes, while the woman says she must do something about S.'s clothes, of course, and that S. can put her things away, lock them up, if she likes, have them back when she leaves or can

sell them, though these days one cannot get much for second-
hand things, or even burn them, so that S. sees herself in a fox
fur stretched out by the pool, sipping Pimm's, but the woman
says she will get her something in white with buttons, the woman
bending over S. so that S. has difficulty thinking of anything
except of this woman, oddly elongated, gaunt, and unnatural,
brushing her body against S.'s knee, and when S. glances up at
her oval face with its even features and white-tipped eyelashes,
it glimmers moonlike, S. thinks, as she closes her eyes, half-
asleep, a cloying scent filling her with a vague note of unex-
pected hope mingled with dull fear, as the woman picks up a
scarf from the floor and pulls the stuff through her fingers,
muttering about some poor thing, and S. rises, barefoot, surveys
the tamed land, a replica of an English garden glimpsed on
some guided tour, she thinks as she glimpses a shadow that may
be the man's, and the land darkens, while the woman blinks her
glittering eyes and mentions an emolument much exceeding S.'s
modest measure, and asks, could they start by getting their teeth
into something substantial?

8) The Days

The swiftly slipping days seem all the same to S.; at breakfast
on the enclosed veranda off the dining room she sits between the
husband and the wife, who call upon her to pass what they
require, while the manservant brings in the scrambled eggs, the
toast, the lamb chops, the kippers or haddock, the tomatoes,
bacon, and sausages or kidneys in covered dishes, and a heaped
bowl of tropical fruit, S. watching the woman serve herself
liberally, but hardly touch the food, pushing her plate toward

S., for S. to consume what remains and then asking S. to accompany her to the woman's room to nurse the woman's migraine, the woman stretching out on the chaise longue, and S. laying cold compresses on the woman's eyes, massaging the woman's temples gently until the woman recovers; S. then writes the woman's letters in a round hand on the scented paper, jasmine, heliotrope, or rose, in the uncertain sentences that the woman dictates, though S. never sees anyone post the letters, nor does S. ever see the man occupied by any employment or avocation, so that S. concludes he is wealthy enough not to work, like many people she has heard about in the city on the high plateau who have made their fortunes extracting minerals from the earth, or is the man flawed in some way and unfit for labor, S. wonders, watching him stroll into the garden in his panama hat and his dark glasses, apparently not even looking about him until S. descends from the closeness of the woman's room to the glittering pool, wearing the black racing costume provided by her employers, of such thin stuff it adheres to her like a second skin, all the more as she swims around the circular pool, knowing that somewhere in the trees the man is watching in his panama hat and his cream jodhpurs, so near to the pool that she sees the man's reflection in the smooth water, while his wife waits in her shuttered room upstairs for S. to return.

9) Accusation

S. finds the table cleared and the man in what appears to be a hunting suit with pockets, a belt, and leather boots, though S. has never seen the man go hunting, nor is there anything to hunt on the land apart from birds, as far as S. knows, the man waiting on the screened veranda, walking up and down desultorily, calling out to S., who prepares to sit at the table, that breakfast is over, asking S. to sit down beside the potted fern, its fine fronds like a web, S. thinks, while the man says he feels it is his duty to let S. know that certain facts have come to his ears, whereupon S. says that someone has been telling untruths, that S. has perhaps glossed over certain parts of her past but has never committed any crime, feeling the soft leaves of the potted fern touching her cheek, but the man interrupts, saying that he has, naturally, no interest in S.'s past, in fact insists that no mention of S.'s past be made, but that he has taken it upon himself, this strictly between the man and S., to let her know that it is not necessary to preserve the fictive account she has offered or to provide any other, that he already possesses more facts than he would have wished, that he will keep this to himself for the time being, and should S. prove by her conduct that the facts that have been revealed to him are of no significance, he will not attempt to use them to blacken her name, but, should he be called upon to furnish a reference before she has proven herself, he would, of course, be obliged to bring them up, though he trusts that he will not be brought to such a tiresome necessity, and certainly S., so far, has given no sign of anything approaching criminal behavior, adding that one never knows of course, but that S. seems diligent enough; in fact, the man can say that he is quite pleased with S.'s performance so far, that he has grown quite fond of S., and, being a man of the world, understands that such things can happen when one is young and impetuous, the man coming over to where S. sits on the edge of the upright chair beside the potted fern and putting his hand on her

shoulder, the man saying that he hopes S. will merit the trust
he places in her.

10) Tennis Coach

S. hears him through the open window of her room in the
middle of the afternoon, crunching the pebbles of the
driveway, coming on rapidly, racquets under his arm and
tennis balls in his hand, a short, wiry, curly-haired man who
occasionally plays tennis with S.'s employer while S. and the
woman sit in the white deck chairs and watch, as S.'s
employer, in long trousers and a white shirt and a baize visor,
plays on the sand-colored court with the morning glory growing
up the wire, the employer hardly moving, only hitting the balls
within easy reach but hitting hard, precisely, almost viciously,
S. thinks, so that the tennis coach is obliged to run rapidly and
sweats heavily, while the employer always drifts off the court
looking as cool as when he went on, every white hair in place,
pouring himself a large glass of lemonade, tilting back his
handsome head to sip from the glass slowly; but often the
employer does not play at all, tells S. she may take the lesson,
and when S. demurs, he says that he prefers to watch, so S.
plays with the coach, who makes S. run back and forth for the
ball until she is tired out, flushed and breathless, the employer
calling out the score in his toneless voice, occasionally giving
S. an unmerited point, it seems to S., though, despite this
help, S. never beats the coach, who winks at S. as they pass
one another, while the couple sit on the lawn watching the
game in their dark glasses, their heads turning slowly together,
as though pulled by a string, S. thinks, until the game ends,

and S. stands wiping the perspiration from her face and neck and shaking hands with the coach across the net, feeling the coach hold her small damp hand longer than is necessary and look S. directly in the eye, though by then S.'s vision is misted with perspiration, and her head is spinning, and she is not certain if it is just the light of the sun setting so brilliantly that she sees reflected in the eyes of the coach, and besides, S.'s employer stands near, waiting and watching, not entering into the conversation, but, it seems to S., listening, while waiting to pay the coach, the folded money ready in his gold moneyclip, so that the conversation never lasts for more than a few minutes before S.'s employer begins counting out the notes visibly, and the coach drops S.'s hand.

11) Maidservant

S. and the maidservant sit on the lawn in the shade and eat figs as dark as the servant's skin, speaking the tongue S. learned before any other while playing sticks and stones in the earth with the dark children; S. tells the maidservant about the farm where the sugarcane ripened in the sun, about the days spent on the dark sand, and the maidservant nods her head and clicks her fishlike tongue and tells S. that she, the maidservant, told her daughter to keep her legs crossed—the maidservant crosses her fingers in the air—but the daughter now has twins, two identical girls the maidservant has to clothe and care for on her day off, paying for their schooling and what's more their school uniforms, and why they have to wear uniforms is beyond her understanding, with the price of things these days, and sometimes S. interrupts to ask about the couple, to which the servant

replies that she knows, ah, what she has seen and heard, that
servants know their masters' secrets without listening at any
keyhole, though what it is she has seen and heard, as far as S.
can understand, has to do with the distant past, the servant
speaking of the first Madame, who, like the present Madame,
came from overseas, and when S. presses, the servant's face
resembles a wooden mask, but when S. asks the servant to show
her the room where S.'s predecessor slept, the servant leads S.
up the stairs slowly, breathing heavily, as she climbs to the top
of the house, to the chamber that seems to S. more comfortable
than the one where S. sleeps, though furnished in a different
style with a large fireplace, padded armchairs covered in chintz,
and over the mantelpiece a painting that appears to be of both
the inside and the outside of the house, views into the rooms that
show the French furniture and even in one room what appears to
be the silhouettes of two figures embracing, and below the painting S. finds a small wooden box with a lock of pale hair tied with
a faded ribbon, and as S. stares at this she hears the door open
and feels a draft and someone behind her, watching her, someone who is not the old maidservant, and when S. turns, she sees
the long phantomlike figure of the woman, who asks with a
gesture if S. would prefer this room, but S. says she is quite
content where she is.

12) The Gowns

In the fine summer dusk S. watches the woman open her closet
and slip her gowns along the rod with a whisper of splendid
stuffs: tulle, organdy, satin, chiffon, pure linen, velvet, in the
muted colors the woman apparently prefers, silver grays, dusky

pinks, pallid blues and lilac, S. smelling the drowsy perfume
that emanates from the gowns until the woman asks S. if she
does not consider *this one is you,* and helps S. undress,
unfastening the mother-of-pearl buttons of S.'s white dress,
telling S. to stand still as S. fidgets in her half-petticoat before
the mirror and, as the woman drags the pale green dress slowly
over S.'s head, S. is unable to think what she is or even of her
name, as though she might not be there at all, as though the
breath has gone out of her and her past gone with it, as the
woman drags the green silk of the dress slowly down over S.'s
plump hips and thighs, S. gasping that it is lovely, but if she
may be so bold as to suggest, a little too tight, and hears the
woman pant with the effort and sees the perspiration glisten on
the woman's pallid brow in the looking glass as the woman
stands pressed against S.'s back, staring at her in the
three-way looking glass, the woman's fine hair cut short and
brushed back from her high forehead, her face heavily
powdered, her eyebrows plucked into such fine lines they are
almost invisible, her eyes darkened with kohl, her lips
carmine, the woman saying she used to be exactly S.'s size,
letting her hand linger with what seems regret on the swell of
S.'s breasts, making S. sit down on the tapestried stool before
the dressing table and taming S.'s thick eyebrows into neat
arches, applying pale foundation to S.'s skin, powdering S.'s
cheeks with a fluffy powder puff, saying that this will take the
roses out of S.'s cheeks, outlining S.'s deep-set eyes with kohl
to bring them out, the woman says, twisting S.'s heavy hair up
into a thick coil at the nape of her neck, pronging the hair with
hairpins the woman holds between her lips, catching S.'s skin
so that S. cries out, spraying S. with her perfume, pressing the
bulb of the vaporizer hard, as though, S. thinks, S.'s odor is

unpleasant, fastening a thick gold slave bracelet around S.'s forearm, and telling S. it is hers to keep.

13) Receptions

Through French doors flung open, S. gazes at the guests drifting across the lawn, crying out greetings, embracing one another; the servants in white uniforms with red sashes barring their chests slant-wise passing around champagne, filling glasses with one gloved hand, the other held behind the back as if, S. thinks, they were wounded; and the couple, he in white tie, she in silver, greet the guests, while S. plays the piano, plays variations of ancient lamentations, singing without reading the score, without separating the notes, the songs the couple has asked her to sing in her slightly flat voice, and watches the guests, who, S. supposes, have made fortunes from the metals of the earth, as they hover around the trestle table, covered with a white cloth, where platters with cold meats in aspic, salads, custards, trifles and jellies, huge bowls of flowers, and piles of gold-edged china and shining silver are lined up in rows, and sometimes the men wander inside, sleeking down their hair, leaning on the piano, offering cigarettes or filling S.'s glass and occasionally, though she protests, slipping money under the music or asking her to meet them in the dark of the garden, and if a circle of them forms around the piano or if one of them sits on the piano stool, the employer draws near to tell them to let her have air, or to tell S. to rest, so that S. sits among the guests and hears a lady, who mops her brow with an embroidered handkerchief, ask what became of the last one, and the man replies that the girl rather lost her head, and once the lights fail and silence falls upon the guests until S. tells them that they need not fear and rushes down the corridor, finding her way by memory, and as she runs back with the yellow candles flickering, feels herself grasped about the waist and pushed back against the wall, as the candles are snuffed, and she becomes aware of a cool hand sliding down her neck into her bodice; then on her hands and knees she fumbles for the candles, pawing the rough pile of the Oriental runner, as a tongue seems to flicker against her skin, a hand lifts her skirt, and S. hears the silk whisper as the hand strokes her thighs, glides between her thighs, and S. leans back against the wall and cries out as the lights return a moment later—she thinks it is a moment later, for she has lost all idea of time— and S. finds herself in the corridor alone.

14) Night

S. wakes, seems to see a double moon, the room dead-still as she sits up in the shimmer of pallid light, asks who is there, and hears that there is no need to be afraid, and lights the lamp, studies the man, his cheeks powdered, it seems to her, his eyes outlined with kohl, his lips glossed, wearing a silk dressing gown, and the woman's yellow scarf, whereupon he lights a cigarette, and S. rises, though the man says that it is better for her not to leave, but she goes into the corridor, switches on the light, thinks she hears footsteps, returns to the room, shuts the door, night in her eyes, the man no longer visible, only the position of the furniture more or less visible, and S. hears the man whisper that he wishes to know everything his wife says, that it is to be S.'s special business to tell him what his wife says, that he entrusts his wife to S., that S. must brood over her, protect her, and love her like a child, S. will know how, but S. replies that she thinks it would be better if she were to leave and considers walking past the man and out of the house but considers also that if the man attempted to stop her there would be nothing she could do, because any kind of struggle with the man would be humiliating, and she wishes to obviate any further humiliation, so she decides to sit down on the chair, but cannot because the man appears to occupy that place, whereupon she lies on the bed and tries to concentrate, but finds she is watching the wan stars in the firmament, falling asleep, until the man shakes her by the shoulder, and S. hears him complain that she is willful and unyielding and demands that she tell him what he has asked, the man hectoring, saying that he only asks for the woman's words, a one-way conversation, and S. stares as the man seems to take a volume from the pocket of his dressing gown, S. making an attempt to repeat something, while the man appears to write in the book and whispers that it's of the *utmost* importance, so that S. tells the man his wife says she is sad, and as S. says these words, she thinks of the wife's sorrow as not only a mortal but a contagious disease, and the man asks if the woman says why she is sad, but S. says no, and the man says that S. must learn everything, and she falls asleep, not sure what the man has said to her, or even if he ever came into her room.

15) Reading

In the heat of the afternoon S. reads words that seem remote, detached, like heavy stones that she drags across the blanched field of the page; she grows confused about who is who, as there

are so many characters and so many events in the book, and she
thinks her life, though half-forgotten, more interesting than
these words; she would prefer to tell the woman, or even the
man, about the place where the sugarcane ripened in the sun,
about the beach where she spent her days lying on the hot dark
sand, rather than read about events that happened long ago in
another country to invented or half-invented people whose
names she cannot pronounce, but the woman acts, S. thinks, as
though S. had not existed before her arrival in this place or
existed only as the perpetrator of some crime or only as an
emanation of the woman, and S.'s past seems to mean much less
to the woman than the words *"All through that night the conversation continued ceaselessly and seemed to consist of the contents of a volume of Gothic tales: before Count Babinski had
finished one direful tale, someone else had begun to relate something still more direful,"* which S. reads, her head beginning to
fall on her chest, whereupon the woman asks why she is falling
asleep over the greatest, the most sublime novel ever written,
and S. looks at the woman lying stretched out across the chaise
longue, cold compresses on her eyes, and begins with *"All
through that night the conversation continued,"* ceases again,
and the woman asks why S. appears so fatigued, whereupon S.
says she thinks the woman's husband came to her room in the
night, and the woman says that she and S. have a covenant, and
that she has been good to S., and that she wants S. to tell her
exactly what happened, to which S. says she is very grateful to
the woman, but that she cannot be sure, whereupon the woman
wants to know is S. absolutely certain that all the husband
wanted was to talk, and is this the truth, the woman lying with
her hand to her head and saying that she has such a migraine,
that she gets no peace at all, that no matter what she does for

people they always take advantage of her, whereupon S. says
that if the woman wishes her to leave she will immediately, but
the woman asks how S. could consider leaving her after all she
has done for S. and weeps while S. reads.

16) Watching

S. feels she is being watched, thinks she hears the thud of a
stone against glass, and runs down the stairs, but once in the
pines sees nothing but long-stemmed trees holding their heavy
heads against the sky and beneath the trees the marble busts,
copies of Roman busts, anonymous heads of the long dead, she
thinks, as she sees someone coming through the trees but hardly
recognizes him until he speaks, coming up to S., who says she
can only stay a moment, that the woman will be waiting, but the
coach sits down so close to S. she cannot move, pressed against
the arm of the bench, as he says he knew she would come to
him, that he knows S. is always watching him from the moment
he walks up the driveway, though she never speaks to him or
even calls him by name, and S. feels his arm along the back of
the bench, while he says he knows she likes him, and S. lets
him put his arm around her, stares up at the bust with the
broken nose and smells the pine trees, and quizzes him about
the couple, until the coach asks why she is always thinking
about them and says S. would do better to think more about
herself, to which she replies that she has more influence than
may be apparent, that she will use any weapon at her disposal,
but the coach responds that despite his station he knows more
about the matter than she thinks, that she is not playing the
game cleverly, stroking her neck as he tells her to get what she

can and then escape as soon as she has an alternative, and even then it will be difficult without his help, he says, settling her on his knees so that she can feel his heat, saying that although his connections are not as good as they used to be, he would certainly do his best, that he still knows some influential people and she must trust him and not be so melancholy, that he is sure she has a photograph of the sweetheart who has made her suffer—or perhaps it is she who made him suffer?—whereupon S. feels the coach slip his hand into her pocket and withdraw the photograph of the young man standing feet apart before the store, a goose at hand, gazing at the photographer through dusty sunlight, as the coach says that the sweetheart, if he is still the sweetheart, is a pretty boy, but does S. imagine he could get her out of her predicament and has she not forgotten him.

17) Caught

S. hears distant thunder rumbling, sees clouds gather and lightning dart as she runs through the pine trees, slipping on fallen needles, passing the anonymous heads as the rain falls hard; she lifts her gaze to the windows and thinks she sees someone watching, so that she runs on faster and is about to enter the hall when she feels someone grasp her about the waist and hears someone ask how she could go running out there to that man, who, surely she must know, is an employee and a common little man besides, and has she lost any power of judgment she may have had, and was she not able to see for herself that the man was of a highly questionable character, and if she absolutely had to go running after the first man that came along, could she not have limited her activities, at least, so that the woman would have been spared certain details, and no, not to say a word, that S. has already said far too much and should learn to be more reticent, that much of what S. says does not redound to her credit, and why did she have to stay away for so long, even obliging the woman to look for her in this terrible downpour, that naturally, if she had been discreet, being a woman of the world, the woman might have overlooked a slight delay, but remaining out there so long, rubbing herself up against that man like a little animal, and not to lie to her, that will get S. nowhere, because the woman has seen all, and besides S.'s thoughts are written all over her face, S. is as transparent as glass, while the rain falls down thickly about them, and the lightning darts on the horizon, hard bright bursts like gunshot, S. thinks, showing the woman's face dead-white, and S. hears the woman say that she has seen the whole thing from the window, and a most disgusting display it was, while the woman sat in her room waiting, her head aching quite intolerably and entirely alone, listening for the sound of S.'s footsteps, she who has S.'s best interest at heart, and after all she has done for S., hoping she could change S., but S. has proved to be more willful than the woman had thought she would be, and the trouble is that the woman has spoiled S., has grown too fond of S., and the woman will most probably catch her death, as she is, as S. can see, wet to the skin.

18) Early Morning

S. wakes with a start in the very early morning, thinks she hears the man call her name, sees the faint light of day and a figure standing by the window in a dark silk dressing gown, the yellow scarf tied about the neck like a tie, the face blurred by sleep and makeup, so that, for a moment, S. thinks it is the woman by the window, and as the sun rises and the garden gathers its daily radiance, the leaves of the trees shining, she thinks, like small polished knives reflecting the sky, she hears the man ask if he may lie down beside her, as he cannot sleep alone, and that she cannot possibily conceive of how weary he is, and will she let him do it to her, just with his hand, and if she will not he does not know what he might feel obliged to do, not that he would want to hurt her, whereupon S. tells him to leave her alone, to go away and leave her alone, and turns to the wall and falls asleep, if she was not asleep before.

19) Misdemeanor

S. oversleeps and misses breakfast, sips from the bottle of wine, picks up her swimsuit, and walks through the orderly house, everything still except for the light hum of the servants' voices in the kitchens, when the old maidservant calls out that S. is to go up to the Madame's room immediately, and S. follows the maidservant onto the veranda off the blue bedroom, where the woman lies stretched out on the chaise longue, sighs, and says that she is not very surprised, that she has been expecting something of this sort for some time, asking if S. has some explanation, whereupon S. says that there is nothing to explain, that if, despite S.'s efforts, the woman is dissatisfied, then S. will leave that afternoon and would it be possible for the woman to pay her and provide her with a reference, but the woman sits up and says that she has no intention of dismissing S., but only of trying to improve her conduct, and that she, the woman, could relieve S. of some of her duties if they are too onerous, but that S. must realize, if she decided to leave now, it would be impossible for the woman to give her a good reference, that as an honest employer she would be obliged to mention the fact that there has been serious trouble of some sort, not only in S.'s past but in the present, that the woman would, naturally, have to mention that S. was not able to rise on time for her duties, and that, obviously, after what has occurred, the woman would have to mention something about it, and that if she, the woman, were in S.'s position she would think twice about her conduct, that there is no point in upsetting the woman, who has come to love S. like her own child, as S. catches a glimpse through the window of the man leaving, and the woman begins to weep, rises from the chaise longue, takes S. by her hands, kisses her softly on the mouth, the cheeks, and on the forehead, and whispers that she will never have any children, that this place will be sold to strangers.

20) Waiting

S. lies in the dim light, smoking cigarettes, drinking heavy red wine, and watching the night-falling sky, the stars crowding, it seems, the heavens, stars that glitter closely above her like a jeweled net, while S. supposes the woman has sent her to her room to torment her, but decides, staring out the window at the glittering sky, that she is not prepared to give the woman such satisfaction, and S., keeping the shutters of her room open so that she can lie in the fierce light of the moon, waits for the sound of the man's car, then leaves her room and walks up and down the narrow passageway as the man climbs the stairs, when

she calls out to him as he makes his way, walking wearily, she
thinks, as he goes along the corridor toward his bedroom, where
he stands with one hand on the door, as S. asks to speak to him,
her words sounding strange to her, dubbed words, or the words
of a much-repeated prayer, or even someone else's words, words
to which he replies that she certainly may but adds that obviously they cannot talk here in the middle of the corridor where
they might wake his wife, whom he would be loathe to disturb,
but that S. may come inside his room, but S. demurs, says she
would like to speak to him in the study or the lounge, where it
would be more appropriate, whereupon the man replies that he
is tired, and that he should not have allowed her to take such
liberties with him, that, surely, whatever she has to say to him
can wait until morning, that he is not prepared to descend the
stairs at this hour, but that should she find what she wants to say
to him sufficiently pressing, she may come back to his door,
which he will not lock, should she desire to come in, so that S.
goes back to her room, undresses, climbs into bed, but is unable
to sleep, rises again and walks up and down, thinking of what
happened in the woman's room that afternoon.

21) In the Man's Room

In the flickering light of the fire S. sees a leather armchair, a
narrow bed in an alcove by the gloomy fireplace, and an armoire
with mirrors on the doors, where the man's lithe body is dimly
reflected as he gets up and locks the door behind S., whereupon
S. says she will only stay a moment and speaks of what occurred
in the woman's room, but the man interrupts, sits down in the
armchair, and tells her to sit by the fireplace on the edge of the

bed, where S. perches uncomfortably in the sultry heat, relinquishing her shawl and unbuttoning her dress at the neck, asking if it would be possible to open a window, but the man says he likes a fire at night even in summer, and that it is never too hot for him, that she should sit farther back on the bed, and as she does so, she says that it is quite unjust that she is being accused of misconduct, after all she has had to put up with, raising her voice, clapping her hand down hard on the striped blanket, her head swimming as she talks, until the man draws his chair closer to the bed and says she is not to excite herself and leans across to place his fingers on her lips before she can stop him, the man warning she will wake the servants, and as the man says this, S. thinks she hears someone cough in the hall, the man raising his voice to say that his wife will do as he tells her to do, taking S. by the hand, telling S. that she is not making things easy for him but that he is willing to make some testimonial, to commemorate her acquiescence in some way, adding that the woman, too, will then surely come around, that S. is not to let her imagination carry her away, but S. cries out loudly, asking the man to open the door, to give her some air, the heat growing, the man's blurred form looming, no, saying no, the quick twist of the scarf about her neck, staring at a gaunt shadow in the mirror, the scarf growing tighter, while S. can see the moon falling and falling through the sky.

22a) Rondavel

S. goes past the twice-bloomed roses, the petals falling softly to the ground, past the pool where leaves drift softly across the water, and comes to the wooded area that surrounds the rondavel, where S. seems to hear a susurrus of voices from behind the door, whereupon she enters and stands within the white-washed walls and gazes as though hypnotized; seeing the figures of the woman and the man in such direct, pitiless light, S. can hardly make out which is the woman and which is the man, the naked bodies anonymous in their perfection, but at the same time smooth, lambent, infinitely desirable, S. seeing the figures perched above the brick-hard earth, sitting on the canvas chairs, ordering S. to remove her clothes, to lie down, speaking fast, the words seeming to flow from the figures endlessly, a hurling sound, a breaking of limits, inundating S., so that S. is caught up in the rush of words, the words surging and breaking like a wave, falling, mounting, rippling, so that she seems to swim in words lasciviously, shamelessly, the words seemingly inside and outside, washing over her as she lies and stares up at the thick beams, listens to the words, and then stares at her own body, lit up in the phosphorus of white light that falls in a single shaft through the high window, the body that seems anonymous in its perfection, someone else's body, belonging elsewhere, S. thinks, as she listens and performs what the figures tell her to perform, every opening filled with the words, the figures speaking metaphorically at times, it seems to S., pompously, pretentiously, the language growing increasingly precious, almost incomprehensible, so that S. no longer listens but only stares up into the beams at a lizard lying motionless as if stuffed, in the shadow of a beam, and then listens anew to the words that seem to lapse into sudden crudity, the words lacerating but spoken in a monotonous flat voice, almost, S. thinks, as though the figures were reading from some manual on the art of loving, ordering S. to combine certain postures in ever-increasing complexity, like a sentence, she thinks, as she lies on the floor, listening to the wind in the larch leaves.

22b) Rondavel

As the afternoon wheels past with the cicadas screeching, S. lies flat on the brick-hard earth, the words dinning in her ears, until she feels the damp floor and hears the wind moan loudly in the trees, and she sees the sky hang low, animate and brooding, and she looks up into the thatched roof of the rondavel and sees a lizard with a new green tail scamper across the thatch and hide under a beam, whereupon the man or the woman tells S. to rise, that they will now lie down on the earth, that S. must now put some order into their proceedings, and S. watches as the figures move slowly, S. gazing as the remorseless light catches their shoulders, her round perfect breasts, the strong muscles of his long arms, the pale hollow chest, the long white girl-legs, the flat stomach, the pubic hair, the penis, the tight buttocks, the arch of a back, as they turn like dancers, silent now, inaccessible, fluid, infinitely desirable, S. thinks, as she rises and sits in the canvas chair and suggests that the man lie down in such a way, that he touch the woman in such a way, enumerating the postures, the places permitted, speaking in her schoolgirl voice, her words gradually surging and breaking like a wave, falling, mounting, rippling, so that the man and the woman seem to swim in her words lasciviously, shamelessly, the words seemingly inside and outside, washing over them, and then S. finding herself lapsing into sudden crudeness, lashing them with words, stinging, scourging them with words, her words like a birch rod or a crop, she thinks, watching the man and the woman with delectation as she combines certain operations in ever-increasing complexity, insatiably, her demands inexhaustible, commanding them to occupy simultaneously all the sites of

pleasure, like a sentence, S. thinks, with expansions, subordi-
nates, determinators, permuting and repeating the acts in her
soft, slightly monotonous voice, while the wind blows hard as a
knife in the leaves of the larch trees.

A Note About the Author

Sheila Kohler was born in South Africa, schooled in France, and now lives in the United States. She is the author of the novel *The Perfect Place*. Her short fiction has appeared in *The Quarterly* and has been reprinted in *Prize Stories: The O'Henry Awards*.